Moonstruck
AND MURDEROUS

First Edition
Printed and bound in the USA

Pen-L Publishing
Fayetteville, Arkansas
www.Pen-L.com

ISBN: 978-1-68313-200-4
Library of Congress Control Number: 2019931493

Cover and interior design by Kelsey Rice

Moonstruck

AND MURDEROUS

~NED McNEIL MYSTERY III~

BLANCHE DAY MANOS

P

Pen-L Publishing
Fayetteville, Arkansas
Pen-L.com

BOOKS BY BLANCHE DAY MANOS

~ The Darcy & Flora Mysteries ~
The Cemetery Club (I)
Grave Shift (II)
Best Left Buried (III)
Grave Heritage (IV)

~The Ned McNeil Mysteries~
Moonlight Can Be Murder (I)
By the Fright of the Silvery Moon (II)
Moonstruck and Murderous (III)

Dedicated to Matt, Dawn, Sara, and Nathan Manos
and to the memory of my parents, Bob and Susie Day.

Chapter 1

Hanging up the phone, I looked down at my dog Ulysses. "That was totally unexpected. Who'd ever have thought I'd get a call from the grand dame of Ednalee, Oklahoma?"

I plopped down on a kitchen chair to think about the strange telephone conversation. In the first place, the call had been from Evangeline Carver. Evangeline Carver! She was a person from my past, long past. This was the first contact I'd had with her since returning to my hometown. She had figured only briefly in my life during the time my family and I lived here, forty years ago. She was a part of the history of Ednalee, a fixture, sort of like our ancient county courthouse or the two-hundred-year-old cottonwood tree out at the river. The Carver family and their huge estate had been in place since long before the Civil War. That Evangeline should call me and, to top it off, ask a favor of me was sort of like a bolt out of the blue. Unexpected.

When I was in the fifth grade, our class, including my friends Pat and Jackie, made a field trip to the Carver farm. Our teacher had thought it would be good, in our study of American history, to see what a huge, thriving enterprise like Carver's looked like, even though it had undergone some changes to keep up with the times. I remembered the long drive up to the house and the fields which grew acres of soybeans. Sleek, pampered racehorses grazed in lush green pastures, and an enormous garden and orchard provided for the family as well as supplying vendors for miles around.

During this school field trip, we were allowed to see the guest or servant's quarters, the smokehouses, the spring house and the clear, cold creek that ran through it, the barns, and the gorgeous flower gardens that surrounded the house. I remembered getting lost in the boxwood maze and the panic that threatened to overcome Pat and me until Jackie, our levelheaded and calm friend, guided us to freedom.

"Just take every right-hand turn," Jackie had told us. "Keep your hand on the right wall and follow those exits."

Pat and I, who were almost senseless from fright, could barely recall which hand was the right one. But, following Jackie's advice, we got out.

"How do you know so much, Miss Smarty?" Pat had asked when we were safely outside.

Jackie just smiled and tapped her head. "I researched it," she said.

Evangeline Carver must have been near middle age at that time. And, if she wasn't royalty, she was near enough for my active imagination. She had come onto the porch to greet us and I was suitably impressed with her regal bearing and lovely clothes. But that was all the contact I ever had with the family.

And now, Evangeline had invited me to come to the Carver home. She asked me to come after supper, around seven o'clock tomorrow night. This, she said, would give the rest of them time to clear out.

Who were "the rest of them?" I wondered.

First, she had asked me if I was the former Miss Nettie Elizabeth Duncan, now McNeil. When I said I was, she told me what her phone call was about.

"I've seen your photographic expertise in the paper," she said, her raspy voice still commanding and clear. "That Daisy Stanton is lucky to have you on her real estate team. I want to talk to you about the possibility of taking pictures of my home. I'll explain it a little better tomorrow night. Will you be able to come?"

2

Would I be able? I gulped a few times, found my voice, and stammered that I would be honored.

Ulysses lost interest in hearing about an impending visit to the Carver farm and Penny, my cat, preferred napping to listening. When the phone rang again and caller ID showed my friend Pat's number, I picked up the receiver, eager to share my excitement. But her first words completely took the wind out of my sails.

"Ned, I'm worried about Jackie." Pat paused and my heart rate speeded up.

"Jackie? Why? Is she sick?"

Pat sighed. "No, not really, but she seems so quiet and sad, not like herself at all. I thought maybe if we met at Grandy's for coffee and a good chat, she'd open up and tell us if something is bothering her or if I'm just imagining things."

"I can be at Grandy's in thirty minutes," I said.

Pat Morris and Jackie Murray, the dear friends of my childhood, had welcomed me home when I returned to Ednalee from Atlanta. Forty years ago, we had called ourselves The Three Musketeers because we were best pals and did everything together. We rode our bikes around town and to the library, went swimming, and joined the Girl Scouts at the same time. Even though I had been back in Oklahoma for only a short time, our friendship had picked up where it left off when my parents and I moved to Atlanta. We were still The Three Musketeers. To think that Jackie was not her usually cheerful self was worrying. Surely, it was nothing that a visit to our favorite cafe and a good heart-to-heart chat wouldn't help.

The heady aroma of coffee greeted me as I stepped through Grandy's door. I loved everything about this place—the comfortable booths with actual padded seats, the individual lighting at each table, the low voices of patrons and the clink of cups and saucers, the friendliness of the coffee shop staff. In those long-ago days of childhood, it had been a malt and soda shop. Sodas and sandwiches were still on the menu, but through the years it had morphed into serving specialty coffee. The cheery and cozy atmosphere was the same, but many of the patrons, instead of being youngsters, were a tad older. It was comforting that the shop had aged a bit, as I had. The wait staff was younger than it used to be, but pleasant.

"Hi, Miss Ned," my favorite waitress, Janey, called, looking up from behind the counter. "Your friends are in the back booth with their drinks already. Do you want your usual caramel mocha?"

Smiling, I nodded. "Sure do, Janey. Thanks."

I slid into the seat facing the door, across from Pat and Jackie.

"Want to order lunch?" Pat asked. "It's nearly twelve."

Jackie shook her head. "You two order if you'd like. I'm not hungry."

"Are you feeling well, Jackie?" I asked. Usually, she was carefully made up, every hair in place, but today, she wasn't even wearing lipstick.

And she was grumpy. "Oh, goodness! Of course I'm well. I'm just not hungry, that's all."

Pat looked at me and rolled her eyes.

I smiled at Janey as she set the hot mocha topped with a generous dollop of whipped cream in front of me.

"I don't want anything to eat either," I said. "The coffee is enough. Besides, I think this mug holds my quota of calories for the whole day."

Pat grinned. "Watching calories, are we?"

I took a sip of the hot, sweet brew. "Not really. At least, not as far as caramel mocha is concerned."

Pat was right. Jackie seemed listless. She toyed with her cup, gazing down at it as the coffee sloshed. She looked pale, and her eyes had dark circles.

I spoke to Pat. "How is the prospective grandmother? Are you making a nuisance of yourself, hanging out at Gerald and Coradee's?"

Pat faked an offended, "Well!"

"Not that I'd blame you," I said. "Since they live in my carriage house, it's entirely too handy for me to just pop in now and then. When their baby comes, I'll bet you move in with them."

Pat laughed. "Now, that's one thing I'd never do, but who knows how I'll be when my grandbaby actually arrives this fall."

I nodded. "It is exciting, and I'm sure Jackie and I wouldn't blame you for acting goofy over a grandchild. Right, Jackie?"

Jackie looked up from her cup and I was startled to see her eyes swimming with tears.

"How should I know?" she asked. "I'm not a mother and will never be a grandmother."

Impulsively, I reached over and covered her hand with mine. "I'm sorry, Jackie. I didn't mean to make you sad. Obviously, I don't have children either, but I'm really happy for Pat."

Picking up her napkin, Jackie dabbed at her eyes. "Don't pay any attention to me. I guess I just have the mid-life blues."

Pat shook her head. "No, it's just the time of year. March is so undependable and strange. Warm one day, cold the next, and to top it off, there are two full moons this month."

Trying to give Jackie time to recover her composure, I said, "Yes, I noticed last night that the moon is getting rounder. It'll be completely full in a few days."

"Bad things happen during a full moon," Pat murmured, lowering her voice. "March is not a good month. Remember the Ides of March and what it did for Julius Caesar? Well, don't laugh, but on March 15, I lost my favorite blue blouse—it isn't in the closet, nor the clothes hamper—it just disappeared. My car had a flat tire for the first time in years. And I tried to bake a cake to celebrate Coradee and Gerald's good news and burned the blamed thing! We aren't through with this month yet and who knows what else might happen under a blue moon?"

A ghost of a smile hovered around Jackie's mouth. "You are so superstitious."

Before Pat could respond, I said, "Hey! Good things happen in March too—really surprising things. Let me tell you about a phone call I got."

The news about Evangeline Carver's request got the immediate attention of both women.

"Lucky you," Pat said. "Do you think it would be all right if I came along when you visit Miss Carver? I'd so love to see the inside of that fabulous house."

Jackie frowned. "Silly! Miss Carver wants to talk business with Ned. If you'll notice, she's the only one who was invited."

"I'll ask her tomorrow night if I can bring both of you if she wants me to photograph her estate," I offered. "She probably won't mind."

"I wonder why she wants pictures of her place," Jackie said.

I wiped a dab of whipped cream from my nose. "Yes, that is strange. Why me, and why does she want the pictures? She said she'd explain tomorrow night."

"I understand she's pretty much of a recluse now," Pat said. "She lives out there in that great big old house with just some servants and I think a relative or two. She has her racehorses. Gerald said she's paranoid about those horses—our sheriff, Milo Cordray, and his deputy have gone to the farm several times when she called to report someone prowling around her barn. Once or twice, she even called Cade and Gerald. She's so afraid something will happen to them. She always runs a horse in the Kentucky Derby."

Gerald Mills, Pat's son, was police chief Cade Morris's right-hand man. He was also a fill-in preacher at our little country church, Rose Chapel.

"Cade didn't mention it to me," I said, "but then, I'm sure he doesn't tell me everything."

Pat grinned. "He probably has other things on his mind when he's with you, Ned."

I felt my face burning. Since coming back to my hometown, I had renewed my friendship with Cade, my grade school protector against bullies who made fun of my red hair. That friendship had blossomed into something a lot deeper in the past year. Jackie came to my rescue before I could think of a suitable retort.

"I hadn't thought about her for years until just last week," Jackie said. "She phoned the office and wanted to talk to Ron. I guess he must be her lawyer."

Jackie worked part time in her husband's office. Of course, there was lawyer-client privilege, but what harm could there be in saying positively that Ron was Miss Evangeline's lawyer?

Pat voiced my opinion. "Don't you know for sure, Jackie?"

Jackie glanced down at her cup. "Ron doesn't talk to me that much anymore."

So, this was the reason for my friend's sadness—all was not well with Jackie and her lawyer husband. Why? I had always thought their marriage was rock solid. But, from Jackie's response, I sensed a crack in that rock.

Chapter 2

My thoughts were still on Jackie and Ron as I drove to my appointment with Miss Evangeline the night following our coffeehouse chat. Jackie hadn't opened up to Pat and me after all. In fact, the longer we sat at Grandy's, the more uncomfortable we became. It was evident that Jackie was fighting back tears and would not be sharing her misery with anyone. Pat had called after I got home, wondering what we could do to help. My advice was that we pray for Jackie and wait until she was willing to share with us. What else could we do?

It had been a long time since the school trip to the Carver farm, so I had to consult my GPS to get directions to Miss Evangeline's home and was surprised to see it was not that far out of town. When I was a child, it had seemed like a long, long way.

The sun had set and twilight was shadowing the hills as I turned off the pavement onto the Carvers' private drive. The road my Escape crunched down was gravel and narrow. I felt as if I were in a time tunnel, not to an actual destination, but traveling back into history. How many carriages, horses, and wagons had traveled this secluded lane? It would not have surprised me at all to see a dashing horseman or a buggy filled with ladies in capes and long dresses clattering toward me.

At last, the driveway divided, one branch going to the right, the other to the left. Guessing that one led to the front of the house and the other to the back, I took the right-hand turn. To prove my decision had been a wise one, as I topped a knoll, the mansion rose before me.

Built in the eighteenth century, according to information I found on the internet, the three-story russet brick edifice rose straight and tall, a double chimney at either end. No welcoming porch, as on many southern houses, just clean, straight lines. The roof jutted out above the upper stories, and there was a brick ledge beneath each of the windows.

It looked very much at home in its surroundings, almost as if it had grown there. It was elegant in its simplicity, and lovely, surrounded by shrubs and trees. In a few more weeks, flowers would be blooming all around it. I sat for a bit, just drinking in the beauty of this magnificent home.

I would have to park here and walk the short distance to the front door, but that was no more than fifty feet. The walkway was made of bricks with ferns, hostas, hyacinths, and azaleas crowding both sides. I could imagine how colorful it would be when the flowers were in bloom.

At the end of the walk, four brick steps rose to the front door, which was dark charcoal as were the shutters framing the windows.

No doorbell, but a large brass knocker shaped like a lion's head hung on the door. Just as I raised my hand to knock, the door swung open and Evangeline Carver stood before me, bathed in the light coming from inside the house.

She was a small person, short, gray hair in curls that stood out from her head, dressed in dark slacks and a bright red cotton sweater. She smiled at me for a moment, then reached out a slim hand and grasped my arm.

"Nettie? You are Nettie McNeil, aren't you? I feel as if I know you. Come in. I've been waiting for you."

The only other person who called me Nettie instead of Ned was my neighbor, Ann Decker. But then, Evangeline and Ann were of the same generation, a generation given to more formality.

9

I stepped into the foyer and blinked at the sudden change from twilight to the brilliance coming from a chandelier in the tall ceiling. A small table holding a bouquet of white gardenias and a rose-colored lamp stood against one wall.

Miss Evangeline barely gave me time to say it was nice to see her again before turning and walking briskly down the hall. I followed, trying to take in the grandeur of the house. The floors were wide plank, polished to a soft gloss. Wallpaper in a muted navy blue figure lined the walls of the hall. But, my hostess evidently wasn't letting me linger to admire her home.

"Come on into the kitchen," she flung over her shoulder. "I'm sure you could use a cup of coffee after that drive. Myra has gone home for the day, but I'm a pretty good hand at pouring liquid refreshment. Myra is my cook, you know," she said, going to the cabinet.

The fragrance of freshly brewed coffee met me as I stepped into the remarkable kitchen. The floor was red brick, polished and smooth. Directly in front of me was a huge fireplace, taking up half a wall. It definitely looked original. The bricks were dull and chipped. It had a long walnut mantel. The whole fireplace was wide enough for a person to step into. On one side was a small warming oven and below it, an opening that was filled with wood for the fire. On the other side was an inglenook or sitting area.

I imagined a spit had once stretched across the blaze for the cook to turn a roasting pig or chicken. A tall wooden churn and a polished fireplace set complete with poker, bellows, a copper bed-warming pan, a shovel, and a broom stood on the brick hearth.

Miss Evangeline saw that my eyes were riveted on the fireplace and she chuckled.

"Been there since the eighteenth century," she said, "like the house. There was no way I was going to tear it out when I had the kitchen modernized."

She motioned me toward a wood table. I sank into a dining chair, frankly gazing around at this large, well-lighted room. Miss Evangeline evidently liked wood. The chandelier hung from a vaulted ceiling with exposed beams, dark from age. Two walls of varnished wood cabinets, a granite countertop, a sink under the window, a recessed refrigerator, and an up-to-the-minute stove completed the furnishings. The kitchen had undergone some modernizing in the last two hundred years while keeping the flavor of a couple of centuries past.

"There!" she said, placing a tray laden with a carafe of coffee, two cups, and cream and sugar on the table.

"Help yourself," she added, folding her hands and beaming at me. She waited until I had a full cup of coffee in front of me before pouring her own.

She swallowed a small sip, set her cup down, and smiled. "You probably have a whole lot of questions," she said. "Why did I call out of the blue, why do I want you to take pictures of my home, and, above all, what does the rest of this house look like?"

I nodded, but before I could answer, she went on.

"You don't know me from Adam, Nettie, but I know your family. I especially got acquainted with your dear Uncle Javin and was so crushed when he went to prison. You see, I just knew he couldn't have murdered anybody. Such a gentle, kind soul."

"I had no idea," I managed to say before she was off and running again.

"Yes, well, some things are so far in the past, you know, and dredging them up doesn't do one bit of good—just brings back sad memories. Besides, you were a child when your folks took you to Atlanta, and children don't need to know too much about these things. I was glad when I heard you were back in town. You see, I'm not getting any younger, hard as that is for me to believe, and I need to take care of a few things before I leave this beautiful old farm that has been my family's home for a mighty long time. I called you for a very special assignment, Nettie, because if you are anything like your family, you are trustworthy, and I want what I'm about to tell you to remain just between you and me."

I had a feeling there was no use in responding to Miss Evangeline, because she was what my father used to call "wound up." She wanted me to listen, so that's what I did.

Without warning, she grabbed my arm. I jumped. She whispered, "Shh. What was that? Did you hear anything, Nettie?"

Her grip was so tight, my wrist hurt. Fear shone from her wide blue eyes.

"No," I said, lowering my voice too. The hand that gripped me shook. My mouth went suddenly dry at the abrupt change in her manner.

"You go peek around that corner and I'll look in the pantry." She pointed toward the hall.

Torn between feeling silly and being afraid of what I might find, I did as Miss Evangeline ordered. I saw nothing but the area we had just walked down to get to the kitchen. Something, however, felt different. Maybe it was Miss Evangeline's terror that had communicated itself to me, but I had a feeling of menace, and I shivered, as if a cold breeze had passed through. Was that a muffled sound of some sort? Holding my breath, I listened. A footstep? A creaking floorboard? Had someone been listening to our conversation? A cold prickle of fear ran down my spine as I returned to the table.

Miss Evangeline closed the pantry door and sat down again. "Well?" she asked.

I shook my head. "Nothing."

"This house is so old that a few family ghosts may linger, you know. They are friendly, nothing to be afraid of, but real people—well, that's something else! Maybe I'm just an old woman who is getting confused with age, Nettie, but I don't think so. You see, I'm pretty sure somebody is trying to kill me."

Chapter 3

I dropped into my chair and stared at her. Was she senile? Did she actually believe in ghosts? Was her imagination running rampant?

"Trying to kill you? What do you mean, Miss Evangeline? Surely, no one is trying to kill you."

She nodded. "Oh, I'm afraid you're wrong there, Nettie. I'm worth a lot of money, worth more dead than alive to certain people, and, you see, there have been things happening—strange things."

"What things?" I asked as she paused for another gulp of coffee.

"My little mare, Melanie. She's a small gray. She and I have been best friends for more than two decades and she's as gentle as a lamb. Usually. Well, the other day, she was acting all nervous and skittish, and when I got on her, she started bucking. Lucky for me that Ken, my stable hand, was close. He grabbed the bridle and got me off. He found a long rose thorn embedded in the saddle blanket. Did it get there by accident? I don't think so. Then, just yesterday, when I came in all hot and sweaty from the garden, Myra poured me a glass of iced tea. I took a sip and it tasted and smelled funny—kind of sour—so I dumped it. Myra swore she got it from the pitcher in the refrigerator, but somebody—I don't think it was Myra—somebody put something in that tea that didn't belong there. I'm just glad I smelled it. And last week . . ."

"Wait," I said. I took a deep breath and downed the rest of my coffee in one long drink. "Have you told the sheriff or Cade Morris about your suspicions? Why are you telling me? What does your staff say?"

"That Mr. Morris thinks I'm an old fruitcake anyway. I've had him and his young sidekick as well as Sheriff Cordray out here too many times when I thought somebody had been messin' around my horses. No, I didn't tell the law, and I haven't told anybody in my household. Don't trust any of them. But, I'm telling *you*, Nettie."

"You mentioned when you phoned that there were several people around. Do you have someone living with you? Relatives?" I asked. Her hands on the table were shaking and I longed to cover them with my own, but I suspected Miss Evangeline didn't want sympathy.

As if she read my thoughts, she said, "I don't want you feeling sorry for me, Nettie, or thinking I've gone 'round the bend. But I do want you to believe me. Just yesterday, I tripped coming down my stairs, and if I hadn't been quick about grabbing the banister, I'd have taken a bad fall. When I asked Lila Mae—she's my housekeeper—about it, she examined the place and said it had been waxed. But, she hadn't waxed it, so who did?"

"Would you like more coffee?" I asked, trying to calm her down a little. If she tried to pour, she'd probably miss her cup.

"Yes, thank you. You asked who else was in the house. Well, there's Myra, you know, and then Lila Mae and my right-hand man Ken and his helper Tyler."

She paused and drew a deep breath. "And then, of course, a head gardener, Jules, and two or three others he hires to help with the heavy work outside. They don't live here, but they come every day, all but Ken. He has an apartment in the loft of the barn. He needs to be close to the horses. He's so good with them. Then, there's Elbert, my cousin, and his wife Pearly, and Veda Johnson, another cousin. They haven't always been here—showed up in the last couple of years, destitute, they said, and claiming I needed somebody to look after me—and what could I do? If they needed food and shelter, I sure couldn't tell any of my family they weren't welcome, could I? But just between you and

14

me, Nettie, I thought of vultures circling when they all started coming. And I'm not even dead yet. My kinfolk don't live in the house, they live in the guest house out back. But, all my family come here to the big house for their meals."

It sounded like Miss Evangeline had a small town either living or working on the farm. Did her cousins help with anything? She hadn't mentioned it. "Actually, if you don't trust your relatives, maybe you should suggest they leave," I said.

What a strange story! Was Miss Evangeline losing touch with reality? Was she in danger? And if she was, why?

She motioned with her hand as if shooing away a pesky gnat. "I can't do that. I don't know which one means me harm and, besides, you know the old saying, *keep your friends close but your enemies closer.* It's an honor thing—a Carver never turns away anybody who's needy, especially kinfolk. Anyhow, this is where you come in."

She smiled and nodded. "It seems pretty suspicious to me that my long-lost relatives would just show up when I'm getting along in years. I don't ever want this place parceled out for house developments or any such thing after I'm gone, and none of my kin loves this place like I do. If somebody waved an offer to buy under their noses, they couldn't resist the million or so they'd get for this. I want my farm to stay just like it is after I'm gone."

She paused and cocked her head, as if listening for a moment before she continued. "Ken loves it, and I thought about surprising everybody by leaving the whole kit and caboodle to him. But, he grew up in Kentucky—had racehorsin' parents, and what if he decided to sell this place and go back home? No, I don't trust any of them. With the exception of one or two bequests, I'm willing it to the Oklahoma Historical Society."

She seemed less nervous now, and I silently tried to digest this startling revelation. Leaving it to the state? She must be quite suspicious of her family to consider cutting them out. No wonder she wanted her intentions kept secret. Those who were hoping to inherit would be sadly disappointed.

"Miss Evangeline, all you have to do is make sure this is all covered in your will. Your wishes will be carried out," I said.

She wrinkled her nose. "That's just it, Nettie. I don't have a will, or at least, I haven't had till now. I've been too busy living, but, well, my old heart isn't what it used to be. Even if I'm wrong about somebody trying to kill me, I won't be here many more years, that's just a fact of nature as the good Lord intended. I need to make sure of a few things before my time is up. So, I'm going to make a will."

"My friend Jackie Murray's husband is a lawyer," I began.

"Yes, I've phoned him," she interrupted. "I'm going to see him to-morrow afternoon and get everything done all legal, but I don't want anybody here to know that's what I'm going to do. Here," she said, pulling a paper from her pants pocket. "I've written down what I want you to do—pictures I want included in the brochure. You see, I want a brochure made up for the historical folk to look at, and I've written down a few facts about the house and grounds, things nobody would know but me. This is what I want included, along with the pictures you take. I want your brochure to be what the historical folk use when they open my home to the public, after I'm gone. I want all these acres to remain in one piece."

She thrust the paper under my nose. "Sign right there at the bottom," she directed.

"Sign?" I asked. "Why do you want me to sign anything?"

"'Cause I don't want you backing out. I've made a copy and I've al-ready signed it, so I want you to sign it too. This just says what I want photographed and tells a little about each thing—those pecan and oak trees, for example, they're older'n Methuselah, and that herb garden, the maze—they are all historical and important. Just sign right there at the bottom. I've listed your fee too."

I gasped when I saw the amount she would pay me. I would have made these pictures just for the honor of doing so. After glancing through her directions, I signed. And, I signed the duplicate.

"Now, I don't mind if folk see you taking pictures. That's fine. Say that I've asked you to take pictures for the library to exhibit or some-thing. Just don't tell anyone about my plans for my farm."

"Okay," I said.

Miss Evangeline sighed and leaned back in her chair, more relaxed than at any time during my visit. "As I said, I'm going to see Ron Murray tomorrow and make out a proper will. There's some things I want done that have nothing to do with what you're going to do, quite a bit of money I've got to dispose of, but this takes a load off my mind. If you can, come a half hour or so before sunset to get started taking pictures. I like the light that time of day and the farm will show up best then. You can take more pictures another time, when the sun's out bright. Thank you, Nettie."

So, I was dismissed. She certainly had a forceful manner. But then, she ran a household and a big organization and was used to her wishes being obeyed. I didn't take offense.

She walked me down the hall and surprised me by giving me a quick hug before I went back to my car.

"You're so much like Javin," she said. Then she closed the door.

The sun had set, and moonlight gilded the pathway. The shrubs beside it cast long shadows as I walked toward my car. What a strange and unexpected tale. Already, I was looking forward to tomorrow. It wasn't until I had pointed my SUV toward home that I realized I hadn't secured an invitation for Pat and Jackie to come back to the estate with me.

Chapter 4

Late the next afternoon, before sunset and after I rounded up my thirty-five millimeter camera, I started for the Carver farm with Pat and Jackie in tow. We three had reasoned that Miss Evangeline would have no objection to their coming since she said I could tell others about taking the pictures, just so I didn't give them the real reason. My pals could give me their viewpoints on the best shots of the farm and the angles from which to shoot. Besides, they were dying to see the historic place up close and personal. Even Jackie was more animated today than she had been; she had applied makeup and seemed her usual perky self.

"Do you think Miss Evangeline is paranoid?" Pat asked as I recounted the first part of last evening and Miss Evangeline's statement that someone was trying to kill her.

"She seemed absolutely normal," I said. "She talked ninety miles an hour, but she made perfect sense."

I told them about the three instances when she might have come to real harm.

"Did she go see Ron about her will today, Jackie?" Pat asked.

"I don't know," Jackie said. "I didn't work in the office this afternoon, but she did make an appointment."

"I brought the paper she gave me last night," I said, patting my purse. "It'll help me get the right pictures."

We turned off the main road onto the Carvers' private drive. Soon, the mansion appeared over a knoll. The sun hung low in the west, lighting and warming the old bricks to a mellow glow. It was a charming, lovely scene. So, why did I feel a shiver of apprehension as I looked at it?

Pat gave voice to my feelings. "It's a gorgeous place, but I wouldn't live here if you paid me."

Jackie frowned at her. "What a thing to say! I'd love to call this place home! Why, I can almost see ladies in hoop skirts, carriages coming and going."

Pat turned to me. "Did you say Miss Evangeline believes in ghosts?"

Jackie playfully swatted Pat's hand. "Don't start that 'ghost' business! You don't have to imagine anything. The whole estate is fabulous just as it is in reality."

"You're right," Pat agreed. "I don't know why I said what I did. It was just a sensation, gone now."

I parked and we got out of the car.

"Wait a minute," I said, raising the camera to my face. "I can't resist getting a picture of the mansion now with the sun's last rays behind it. Doesn't it look grand?"

"It looks spooky," Pat muttered.

We trooped up the brick walk to the front door. I banged with the door knocker and we waited.

"That's funny," I said. "Last night, she got to the door before I knocked. I thought she'd be all eager to meet us today and direct me to what she wants photographed first."

Once again, I knocked.

"I hope she hasn't fallen," Jackie said. "Try the door, Ned."

I turned the knob and the door swung open. Instead of being brightly lighted, the entry was shadowy and empty. I went in and called, "Miss Evangeline! I'm here for the pictures."

My voice echoed eerily down the hall. I shivered and stepped back to join Jackie and Pat.

This was strange. I pulled my phone from its holster. Maybe I should call her.

"Listen!" Pat said. "I hear some people talking. Down that way." She pointed.

I heard them too. It was a relief to know we were not alone.

"We'll follow their voices. Miss Evangeline may have been held up by some business with the gardener or someone," I said as I walked onto the graveled path that ran behind the house.

We passed through carefully maintained gardens, beds of iris, an herb garden with a pergola, banks of shrubbery, and the entrance to the boxwood maze. The path led behind guest houses and under towering oak and magnolia trees. Corrals and barns loomed nearby. A half dozen men and women were standing inside the corral fence, talking and gesturing. They sounded upset.

Six pairs of eyes stared at us we walked up to the group.

A tall, angular woman with gray hair that was pulled away from her face into a tight bun turned from gazing off into the distance as we approached.

"Who are you?" she asked, her voice shrill with suspicion. "Do you know where Evangeline is?"

"Miss Evangeline? Isn't she with you?"

"No," a short, balding man said. "No, she isn't, and we're beginning to get worried. Who are you and why are you here? Do you know anything about her?"

My heart speeded up. Miss Evangeline was missing? "I'm Ned McNeil," I said and introduced my friends. "We—um—we have an appointment with Miss Evangeline."

A slim man, a little younger than I, dressed in jeans, boots, and a wide-brimmed hat strode from the barn leading a saddled roan horse.

He tipped his hat. "Sorry if we're not up to being hospitable, ma'am, but we're all kind of worried. Miss Evangeline went for a ride earlier and hasn't returned yet."

"I thought you were supposed to be keeping up with Evangeline when she was out on that mare of hers," accused the short man, frowning at him. "Evangeline isn't young. She shouldn't be allowed to ride at all, especially not by herself. If something has happened to her, I'll hold you responsible!"

The slim man's eyes glinted. "And who's going to tell her to quit riding? You, Elbert? I sure wouldn't. I was busy in the back pasture and thought Tyler, here, could unsaddle Melanie when she got back, so I didn't know Miss Evangeline hadn't come in from her ride until just a while ago."

A blond-haired boy, I guessed him to be in his early twenties, strode to meet me, hand outstretched. "I'm Tyler, ladies, and I work here too, with Ken. I thought that he had tended to Miss Evangeline after her ride and had no idea she was still out till Myra came to say she hadn't been to eat supper."

He looked down at his boots and mumbled, "If I had checked the horse corral and stables, I'd have realized Melanie wasn't here."

A plump, gray-haired woman in a housedress and apron spoke, her voice quavery. "I sounded the alarm when she didn't show up for supper with the rest of the family."

"Are you Myra?" I asked around a lump that was beginning to form in my throat.

She nodded, wrapping her hands in her apron.

The tall, skinny woman sniffed and stared at me. "Just what kind of business did you have with Evangeline anyway? Is that a camera around your neck? We don't allow photographers to go roaming around, snapping pictures and selling them." Her voice reminded me of a fingernail on a chalkboard.

"Now, look," I said, feeling heat start up my neck. "I'm here because Miss Evangeline asked me to come. So, I think you'd better talk with her if you don't agree with her decisions."

The last person in our little tableau smiled and came toward me with her hand extended. "I'm Pearly Carver, Elbert's wife. Our cousin Evangeline is very dear to us, and we are frantic with trying to guess where she might be. Forgive us for being blunt. This is my husband, Elbert Carver." She gestured toward the balding man. "And she," she nodded toward the woman with the bun and caustic attitude, "is Veda Johnson, another cousin."

I shook hands with Pearly, as did Pat and Jackie. Pearly was the most attractive of the group. Her ash-blonde hair was in a short, stylish cut and her makeup subtly enhanced her complexion.

Jackie had backed away from us and pulled her cell phone from her purse. Of course—Ron! Miss Evangeline had made an appointment with Ron. Had she kept it?

Slowly, Jackie replaced her phone and came back to stand beside me. Drawing a deep breath, she said, "Miss Carver was planning to see my husband in his office this afternoon, but she didn't show up."

"An appointment with your husband?" Elbert echoed. "Why? Who is your husband?"

Jackie's eyes met mine and she shrugged. "He's a lawyer."

It was as if an electric shock ran through the Carver family.

"Lawyer?" Veda shrilled. "What would she want with a lawyer?"

Jackie smiled. "That's something you would have to ask her, I'm afraid."

Ken swung up into his saddle. "I'm going to ride over to the north pasture. That's where she usually goes. Surely, she just lost track of time."

"I'll saddle up and follow you," Tyler said, starting toward the barn.

"Wait!" Myra shouted. "Look! Here comes Melanie."

A small, gray mare trotted toward us. Her head was up, and she held it to one side to keep from stepping on her trailing bridle reins.

Ken rode to meet her, and she shied away. At last, he grabbed the reins and led her back to the corral. Silence fell on the entire group. Myra began to cry.

"She's nervous," Ken said. "Melanie is usually the gentlest little mount you could wish for, but she's excited about something tonight. Take care of her, Tyler. I'm going to find Miss Evangeline."

Ken whirled his horse and galloped off in the direction from which Melanie had come.

The riderless mare was not a good sign. My heart was doing double time. I walked over to where Tyler stood holding the quivering animal's reins. Her saddle had slipped, and the saddle blanket was halfway off.

Remembering what Miss Evangeline had said about a thorn in the saddle blanket, I ran my hand along its underside. Nothing there that would startle Melanie. But, what had happened? Why was she, who was usually placid, plainly excited? And where was Miss Evangeline?

Tyler patted Melanie's neck and wordlessly led her into the stable.

"I've got to keep busy," Myra muttered, trotting toward the house. "I'll bring us back some coffee."

"Good idea, Myra. Thank you," Pearly said.

"I'm not leaving this corral until I know what happened to my cousin," declared Veda.

"I'd like to stay," I said to Pat and Jackie. "Is that all right with you?"

"Couldn't drag me away," Pat declared.

"Me neither," Jackie agreed.

Thirty minutes later, Ken returned at a gallop.

"Did you find her?" Elbert asked.

Ken swiped his hand across his eyes and nodded. In a choked voice, he said, "She's lying out there in the grass. Looks like Melanie threw her and she hit her head on a rock. Miss Evangeline—I'm afraid . . . she's dead."

I felt as if someone had sloshed a bucket of ice water over me. My friends and I joined hands, and Pat bit her lip. Evangeline's family stood with shocked, white faces. Myra, newly arrived with a tray and coffee cups, softly sobbed.

"I'm calling an ambulance," Ken said. "It's no use, but I'm calling one."

"Call the sheriff too," I told him. "And I'm calling Cade Morris." No one objected.

Chapter 5

My friends and I stayed until the ambulance arrived with Sheriff Cordray and Cade not far behind. It was as if I couldn't leave until I knew that Miss Evangeline would have someone to look after her, but now, I was free to go home. Silly, I know, but I've never claimed to be completely logical.

I walked over to Cade and grasped his hands. His eyes questioned me.

"Give me a call tonight when you have time," I said.

"Yes," he said, "I'll do that."

Jackie turned to go. Pat and I followed.

The sun had set, and twilight was spreading a soft purple haze across the landscape. The white orb of the waxing moon rose over the Carver mansion. To me, the house looked lonely and empty. Trees and shrubs seemed hushed and still, a rigid sort of stillness. Even the wind had stopped. Generations of Carvers had given this place life and meaning. What would happen to the estate now? Would Elbert take over? Did he have the knowledge to run the huge enterprise? I hadn't known Miss Evangeline long, but I sensed that she was the lifeblood that kept everything moving smoothly. Now that she was dead, it seemed to me that life had gone from the very bricks of the mansion.

We three didn't talk much on the way back to Ednalee. When I reached my house, I asked Pat and Jackie if they'd like to come inside, but they declined. They, as I, just wanted to sit down and try to absorb the awful thing that had happened.

Both my animals rose up from their naps to meet me. I fed them and heated milk for a cup of hot chocolate. I felt chilled to the bone.

A couple of hours later, there was a knock at my front door. As he always did, Ulysses went with me to answer it. Cade stood in the glow of the porch light.

The shock and sadness I had felt since learning of Miss Evangeline's death lessened with the warmth and gladness that Cade's presence always brought.

He gave me a swift peck on the cheek as he came inside the house. Putting his arm around my shoulders, he walked with me into the living room.

"Tired?" I asked as he sank down on the sofa.

He nodded. "Tired and feeling kind of like somebody kicked me in the stomach. Poor Miss Carver. Except for Elbert, the last of a dynasty. After all these years of Carvers at that big old farm, it's hard to believe."

Tears burned my eyes. I nodded.

"Tell me what you were doing there," he said, his blue eyes searching my face.

So, I told him about Miss Evangeline's phone call and the real reason I had been at the estate when he arrived.

He ran his hand across his mustache and shook his head.

"She thought somebody was trying to kill her?" he asked.

"That's what she said, Cade, but she also told me there were probably ghosts of her ancestors in the house. It could be that she had a lively imagination and was getting suspicious as she grew older. Or, maybe she was becoming senile. Did you see anything that might have caused you to believe her death wasn't an accident?"

"It looked like something spooked her mare and she threw her onto some rocks," Cade said, squinting as he thought back. "The mare—her employee Ken called her Melanie—he said usually she was gentle and a good mount for Miss Evangeline. Something must have scared her and she started bucking. The ground was all torn up around where Miss Carver lay. It looks like she probably fell off and hit her head."

"But, you didn't know then that she thought somebody was trying to kill her," I said.

Slowly, he shook his head. "No, I didn't. So, I wasn't looking for anything suspicious."

"If you had suspected it wasn't an accident, what would you have been looking for?"

"Anything that could have spooked the mare. A horse, any horse, can be unpredictable, even a gentle one. Maybe Melanie saw a snake or a wild pig. Ken said they sometimes have trouble with wild hogs rooting around, trying to find something to eat. Surely, it was just an old woman's imagination that made her say someone was trying to kill her. It was a sad accident, Ned, so get that thoughtful look off your face."

I turned toward him on the sofa, tucking one leg under me. "All I'm saying is, maybe we should keep an open mind. Think about it—she told me of three different incidents that could have resulted in tragedy. Those relatives of hers came circling in like buzzards only a few years ago, as if they were waiting for her to die and, Cade, today she was supposed to have met with Ron Murray to make out a will. I think someone was listening when she told me what she wanted done. She was going to leave the estate to the Oklahoma Historical Society, not to any of her family."

He shook his head. "Hmm. I don't imagine any of her family would be keen on that. I don't like the way you said, *we should keep an open mind.* Forget the *we* business, Ned. I'll look into it. If, on the off chance her death wasn't an accident, there is a killer out there who doesn't want Miss Evangeline to leave her home to the state, and he might not appreciate your curiosity."

"She didn't have time to meet with Ron and draw up a will," I said. "What will happen to all her assets?"

"If a person dies intestate, usually the next of kin inherits," he said. "Ron would know a lot more about that than I do. Maybe she had talked with him before yesterday and he knew what she wanted done."

"Maybe." I snapped my fingers. "That paper! The one she had me sign about making a brochure for the Historical Society. Would that have any legal weight?"

"I don't know. Some wills are just handwritten with a signature. It would probably have to have her signature on it, or it wouldn't hold up. Did she sign it?"

"She did. What's more, she insisted I sign it too. She gave me a copy and had another copy that she kept. Surely that would constitute a written will, wouldn't it?"

"I don't know," Cade said. "Let me take a look at it."

I trotted to my purse, rummaged through it, and came back with the folded paper I had taken with me to the farm.

Cade read silently then drew a deep breath. "At the bottom, she wrote 'these are my wishes' and she signed it. Could be a legal document. I think you need to take it to Ron. With his training, he'll know whether this is as good as a formal will."

"You're right, Cade. I'll do that tomorrow morning, if he can see me."

For the first time in this wretched evening, I felt a spark of hope. If Miss Evangeline wanted her home to go to the Historical Society, I would do my best to carry out her wishes. And, before I went to see Ron, I just might take a little jaunt out to the Carver farm. But, how would I see the place where she had died? How would I be able to find it? I would have to figure out a way.

Chapter 6

By morning, I had a plan. As soon as I thought the law office had opened, I gave Ron a call. Jackie answered and I asked if Ron could see me around eleven.

"Do I sense that this is about Miss Evangeline?" Jackie asked.

"Yes, it is, actually. Remember, I told you and Pat that she hadn't made a will? Well, I guess she did, of sorts. She wanted it kept secret, but she's gone now and I don't think the secret part matters. I have a paper she and I both signed. She wanted me to take pictures for the Historical Society. You see, she planned to leave the estate to the Society instead of to her family. I need to know what Ron thinks about it."

"Oh, Ned! That's amazing. The Historical Society? What a disappointment for any of her family who have hopes for inheriting. Ron can certainly give you some advice."

Jackie ascertained that I could see Ron at eleven. After saying goodbye, I sat quietly on my kitchen chair for a minute, finishing my coffee. Jackie was right. The Carver heirs would be furious, probably. Furious enough to keep her wishes from going into effect? I remembered the noise Miss Evangeline had heard when she had me get up and look down the hall. Had someone been listening to her plans?

But, in reality, why should I even worry about it? I should leave it with Ron and forget it. Mixing metaphors, as I was prone to do, I could just let the chips fall where they might, and not dip my paddle into the stream and muddy the waters. Thing of it was, I *did* know what Miss Evangeline wanted done and, like it or not, I had her directions. If possible, I'd like to know if Miss Evangeline's death was an accident.

Swallowing the last gulp of coffee, I got up, gave Ulysses a pat on the head, and told him to guard the house. Penny had eaten earlier and now, undoubtedly, was upstairs curled on my pillow, enjoying one of her long naps.

Grabbing the camera I had left on the table last night, I went out the kitchen door to my car parked in the attached carport Dink Renfro built last year, to my eternal gratitude. Getting in, I drove down my long driveway past the carriage house. Lights in the kitchen told me that Coradee was awake, but Gerald's car was gone so he was probably already on the job. Once again, I thought of how blessed I was to have that young couple so near. Pat's son was a hardworking, trustworthy person, preaching on Sundays at Rose Chapel and studying nights for a law degree. And Coradee, despite the bad reputations of her father and uncles, was a sweet, loving girl.

I aimed my SUV out of town toward the Carver estate. How would I find the exact spot where Miss Evangeline had died? And why was it important that I see it? What did I expect to find? I had no idea how far from the barn it was nor how hard it would be to find or even if I'd know when I found the right place. Although I did not plan to sneak in, the wisest thing would be to keep a low profile, so, after turning off the main road into the Carvers' private drive, I pulled to the side, parked, and got out.

This time, I chose the left fork at the place where the driveway divided. Following it, I walked to the back of the house. As I had guessed, this led to a detached, double-car garage. Still skirting the house, and keeping trees and bushes between me and the guest cottages, I headed toward the barn.

Ken was brushing a shiny black horse standing patiently in the corral. He looked up as I approached.

Not knowing what sort of reception I'd get, I thought I'd better jog his memory.

"Hi, Ken. I'm Ned McNeil, in case you don't remember my name. I met you yesterday, but I didn't catch your last name."

We shook hands, a small grin quirking his mouth. "Ken Riley, ma'am. Of course, I remember. What can I do for you this morning?"

"First, I want to offer my sympathy. You knew Miss Evangeline, maybe for a long time, and I had just met her, but I'm terribly sorry about her death. I wish I had known her longer than a few hours."

"Thanks," he said. "She was a great lady. I've worked here on the farm for a lot of years. Seems impossible she's gone, and having to die like that, just lying on the grass, hurting, well, it's not right. On the other hand, she died doing what she loved—riding that favorite mare of hers."

His eyes narrowed. "As I said, what can I do for you? Did you have some unfinished business with Miss Evangeline?"

Taking a deep breath, I lifted the camera that hung from my neck. "Miss Evangeline wanted me to make some pictures of the farm. That's why I have the camera."

His face hardened and he shook his head. "No, I don't think that'd be a good idea now. Besides, if you wanted pictures, why didn't you stop up at the big house? I imagine those relatives of hers are there, probably deciding on who gets what."

I had told Ken the truth, but not the whole truth, and evidently that wasn't enough. Without knowing whether it was a wise thing to do or not, I decided to state the real reason I was there.

"Actually, Ken, I want to see the place where Miss Evangeline died."

"Why?"

How could I say this without sounding like I suspected her death might not be accidental?

"I just want to see if I can find anything that might look—well—I hope you understand. I want to see if I can find anything at all that might have spooked her horse or caused her accident."

He stroked his chin, his eyes thoughtful as he stared past me. "Uh-huh. I understand that, but I'm surprised you're thinking along the

30

same lines I am. I planned to go back this morning, too, just to look around. Can you ride?"

I grinned in relief. "It has been years, but I think I remember how. None of Miss Evangeline's thoroughbreds, though."

"Nope. Nobody but her jockeys and trainers ride them."

A few minutes later, Ken and I were on horses, trotting through the pasture. He had chosen a pretty sorrel horse for me and he rode the black horse he had been brushing. I found the saddle surprisingly comfortable. The morning was cool but sunny, the fresh smell of springtime was in the air, and I relished the feel of the breeze on my face. If it weren't for the grim destination of our ride, it would have been enjoyable.

We didn't talk much, being busy with our own thoughts. I could imagine Miss Evangeline thinking she would have time for a jaunt into the pasture before meeting with Ron, asking Ken to saddle up Melanie, and perhaps thinking about the things she would include in her will. She probably rode into the pasture as she had done countless times.

Ken pointed out a white board fence in the distance. "That's our racetrack," he said. "Each year, Carver Farms runs a horse in the Derby. That's where they are trained."

I nodded. This farm and her horses had been Miss Evangeline's life. What would happen to it now that she was gone? Would Elbert inherit it? Was he the next of kin? How about Veda? She was some sort of cousin, but would she be included? Would it stay the same or would it be parceled out and turned into something quite different from the lovely place it was now?

Something else was bothering me. "Miss Evangeline went for her ride long before she was found. She must have thought she'd have time for a ride before going to meet her lawyer in town. Why didn't Melanie come home hours before she did?"

Ken smiled. "Melanie had been taught to stand still when her rider dropped the reins. She must have stood where Miss Evangeline fell for a long time until she realized Miss Evangeline wasn't going to move. That's when she came back home."

The terrain changed from smooth grass to a few pines and cedars. The ground was still wet with a heavy dew, and I noticed my horse was stepping carefully, avoiding some rocky patches.

At last Ken reined his mount to a stop. "We'd better walk the horses from here on," he said. "The ground gets rockier. Not a good place to go riding."

I followed Ken, my horse picking his way around rocks.

"Wait." Ken held up his hand and pointed a short distance in front of us.

"This is where she fell."

I slid off my horse and hurried over to a jumble of rocks. "This is where you found her?"

"Yes," he said. "She was lying on those rocks."

I walked over to the pile of rocks and stood looking down. "Do you think her head hit them and that's what caused her death?"

He nodded, his mouth a hard, grim line. "Yes. It must have been. I came back with the ambulance attendants and the sheriff and Chief Morris last night to show them where she was."

"I don't understand one thing," I said, searching Ken's face. "Why did Miss Evangeline ride Melanie onto this rough stretch of ground? Why didn't she stay on the smooth pasture grass?"

"I wondered that too," Ken said. "But, if Melanie had been spooked by something, she probably was hard for Miss Evangeline to hold back. Melanie ran, then she bucked and threw her off."

Glancing at Ken, I found him watching me. "Melanie was terrified of wild hogs, and we've had some trouble with them lately, rooting under fences to get to the crops, so I guess it's possible that one caused her to panic," he said.

"I really don't know what I'm looking for," I said. "Maybe I just wanted to see the place where she died, try to feel a little of what she felt as she took her last ride."

We searched, eyes to the ground, walking in ever-widening circles, but we didn't find traces of hog tracks or anything that might have scared Miss Evangeline's mare.

The ground was plenty torn up. In addition to the tracks Ken's horse and Miss Evangeline's had made yesterday, there were the tire tracks of the ambulance and the sheriff's truck.

Ken walked back to his mount, put his foot in the stirrup, and swung up.

"I don't like it here," he said. "Are you ready to go?"

"I don't much like it either," I agreed. "Yes, I'm ready. I probably shouldn't have come, but thank you for guiding me. It seems so unreal to me that she died last night. I was looking forward to talking with her again. Now, that'll never happen."

Ken shook his head. "No. It never will. Do you want to tell me what you were really doing here last night? Or had you and Miss Eva cooked up some deep, dark secret?"

"She didn't want anybody to know about it, at least for now. I'm sure it won't be long, though, before everyone knows why she asked me here. I wonder if I hadn't come the night before, the night she first talked to me, if she'd still be alive today."

"You've really got my curiosity going," Ken said as we turned our horses back toward the barn. "I don't see how anything she said could have resulted in Melanie running away with her. But, as you said, maybe before long, everybody will know your secret."

My horse suddenly shied and I grabbed the saddle horn to keep my seat. A rabbit darted out from a clump of cedars that I hadn't noticed earlier. Wasn't it strange to have a cedar thicket just sprouting out of the pasture? I reined my horse closer to take a better look.

Without dismounting, I glanced at the ground. Scrub cedars, briars, and sumac bushes crowded together. The grass looked scuffed and, in the dirt, I noticed some prints. Could they be footprints? I was still staring at them when Ken rode up.

"Find anything interesting?" he asked.

I pointed toward the disturbed rocks and partial prints.

"Why would a person be out here among these trees?" I asked.

He shrugged. "Beats me. I wouldn't think anybody would have any business here. Maybe Tyler was here for some reason or another."

I nodded. "Maybe. Wait a moment, Ken. I'm going to snap a picture."

Aiming my camera at the scuffed area, I zoomed in for a close-up and pushed the button.

"So, you think this is important enough to show the sheriff?" Ken asked.

I nodded. "Could be. I want to look at the photo more closely when I get home."

I didn't tell Ken, but I doubted I would share my find with Cade—at least, not yet. He had told me I shouldn't be in on this investigation into Miss Evangeline's death, if, indeed, there was to be an investigation. So far, everyone accepted her death as an accident, but I wasn't sure—not sure at all.

Chapter 7

Ron smoothed the paper on his desk and read it again.

"Miss Carver gave you this?" he asked.

I nodded.

"You signed it. She signed it. It's dated. She told me when she phoned that she wanted to make out a will, but she, of course, didn't get here. I'll check to be sure, but this looks like it would hold up in court, if no one contests it. You said she kept a copy?" Ron glanced from the paper to me.

"Yes," I said. "I signed her copy too, but I don't know where hers is. Somewhere in her house, I assume."

"That's good," he said. "Just corroboration. I think I should keep this locked up in my office, Ned."

"That's what I think too. I don't want the responsibility of keeping it safe."

Jackie had been sitting quietly beside me.

"Have you heard from any of her relatives?" she asked her husband. "I'm afraid this handwritten will may be contested."

"It'll be interesting to know which one of them objects," I interrupted. "Miss Evangeline's death was a little too fortuitous. I'm afraid somebody was listening when she told me of her plans to will the farm to the Historical Society. And before she could come in to see you, she was dead. Do you think I'm letting my imagination run away with me?"

35

Ron smoothed his thinning red-gray hair. "No, I think you're just looking at facts, and no, I haven't heard from any of the Carvers," he said, answering both Jackie's and my questions. "Did Cade find anything to suggest a suspicious death?"

I shook my head. "Nothing at all, but when he and the sheriff went to the pasture, they weren't thinking of a murder."

I told them about the area behind the cedars I had found.

Ron shook his head. "The farm is a big place, Ned. Those tracks could have been there for any number of reasons."

"Maybe the fact that she took me into her confidence, maybe that's just coincidence and there's nothing at all sinister about the timing of her death. But, she thought she heard someone in the hall when we were sitting in the kitchen. I didn't see anyone, but I had this feeling that someone else was in the house. She thought someone was trying to kill her, and she didn't trust her relatives."

Jackie stood. "I'm getting us all a fresh round of coffee. Ned, I don't like the part you have in this. Through no fault of your own, you may be in a dangerous position."

"Because I'm the one Miss Evangeline talked to?" I asked.

Ron answered for her. "From what you've told me, Miss Carver didn't share her intentions with anyone but you. She planned to keep her will secret from her family. Now, why would she do that unless she didn't trust them? You said she thought someone was trying to kill her. Several million dollars could be an incentive for murder for someone who was desperate. Her killer wouldn't want you to carry out her plans for leaving everything to the state and cutting out her family. Your coming to me with this paper should make you safer, if her death wasn't an accident, and if the killer knows you've come to talk to me."

I shivered. "I hadn't thought that someone could be following me."

I warmed my hands around the cup of coffee Jackie brought. "I don't know how anything could be proved about the way she died. I looked at the spot in the pasture. Her mount evidently threw her, but the mare, Melanie, was usually gentle. I'm wondering what spooked her?"

36

Jackie rose to her feet. "I'm going home—got a million things to do that have nothing to do with old ladies or murder. Will you be home for dinner?" she asked Ron.

He shook his head. "No, I'll be working late."

A shadow crossed Jackie's face. I pushed my chair back and stood.

"I should be going too. Thanks, Ron. I'll leave this dilemma with you. I can't understand how anyone could find it in their hearts to murder a sweet, innocent little old lady, if it was murder."

Ron grinned as he reached for his desk phone. "Little and old? Yes. But sweet and innocent? You didn't know the Carvers or Miss Evangeline, Ned. She lived a long time and she had a past, as we all do. You were gone from Ednalee for forty years so you wouldn't have heard any of the stories but, believe me, a lawyer hears them all. That family could be just about as ruthless as anybody you'd ever meet."

Ruthless? Sweet little Miss Evangeline? I didn't want to hear this. Even though I had known her for only a short time, I didn't want my impression of Miss Evangeline shattered—not by Ron or anyone else.

But, Ron told me anyway. "Old Judson Carver, Miss Evangeline's father, was . . . well, the only way to say it is he was a greedy, grasping old rascal. He seemed to enjoy foreclosing on farms. Grew his own holdings that way, by taking what had belonged to others. There was a story that happened way back while Miss Evangeline was young. I don't know all the inside information on it, just what my dad told me. Somehow or other, Judson's older brother Charles disappeared, and Judson came into possession of the Carver farm that had belonged to his brother. I don't remember the details, but the story ran that the brother was so deep in debt, he was about to lose the farm. Public opinion was that he had run out on his debts and Judson paid them off, saving the whole estate from foreclosure."

I shook my head. "What a terrible thing. At least when Charles left Judson holding the bag, the farm wasn't lost. That was good of him to pay off what Charles owed."

Ron smiled and shook his head.

Chapter 8

I did what I always do when I want answers to perplexing questions or simply crave a bit of comforting. I phoned Mrs. Ann Decker, my next-door neighbor.

"I was thinking about you," she said, a smile in her voice. "Would you believe I've just taken a pan of shortbread out of the oven? Come on over and share it with me."

I didn't need to be asked twice. Putting down the phone, I hurried next door. The delicious aroma of fresh-baked cookies led me from Miss Ann's porch into her kitchen.

"Have you heard that Evangeline Carver died last night?" I asked. "I was there at the farm when Ken Riley, her stable hand, found her lying dead out in her pasture."

"Yes, I heard about Evangeline Carver's death," she said as we sat at her table, frosty glasses of iced tea in front of us and warm shortbread on a plate. "I didn't know you were acquainted with her. Death is a sad thing, whether it comes to a young person or an old one."

Miss Ann, soft-spoken and kind, was a trustworthy sounding board for my ideas and a gold mine of information about the people who lived in Ednalee. Her husband, Eldon Decker, had been killed years ago, and my Uncle Javin spent forty years in prison, accused of Eldon's murder. Miss Ann's life had been hard, but she was the sort of person who was easy to talk to. Nothing much shocked her, and she looked at facts through eyes that had seen years of sunshine as well as shadow.

"I knew Evangeline," she said, gazing into the past. "Eva, we called her when we were a lot younger. She always had a slew of boys swarming around her, but she was a flirt. She'd lead them on, then dump them."

Oh, my! A flirt and ruthless? My first and only impression of the lady of the manor might not have been an accurate one.

I nibbled a piece of shortbread. "This is delicious," I said. "Miss Evangeline mentioned Uncle Javin. Said he was kind and gentle and she didn't believe he was guilty when he was charged with murder."

Miss Ann raised her eyebrows and sniffed. "Maybe she didn't believe it, but she didn't exactly stand by him either. To give her her due, though, that was probably her old daddy's doing. He didn't want the family name sullied by her marrying an accused murderer."

"Do you mean Uncle Javin was one of her conquests?"

"I don't know," she said slowly, smoothing away a rivulet of moisture on her frosty glass. "Javin and I were friends and he sometimes confided in me. Being a gentleman, he never directly criticized Eva, but I could tell most of the admiration was on her side. She was right when she said he was kind, and he didn't want to hurt her." She grinned. "Probably didn't want to make her mad either. She had a pretty good old temper."

Finishing my shortbread, I sighed. "Just how friendly were those two?"

Miss Ann dabbed her mouth with her napkin. "I'll give you the recipe for that shortbread if you'd like, Nettie. How friendly? Not sure. Sometimes I suspected too friendly. If she ever visited him in prison, I didn't know about it. Those years he spent in prison in McAlester sort of ended their romance. But, to give her the benefit of the doubt, she never did marry anybody, so maybe she carried a torch. Probably didn't find anybody she could trust. She suspected everybody was out to get her money."

"Uncle Javin never married either," I pointed out.

"No," she agreed. "He never did. If he hadn't been in prison, he might have."

"What else can you tell me? Ron said the family was ruthless. Do you agree? Had you heard the stories about Judson Carver?"

"Of course, I heard them. Gossip is not a new thing, you know. I was never the recipient of old Mr. Carver's meanness. He owned the biggest share in the bank downtown—he was the bank president. I guess Eva inherited those shares when he died. He would sometimes foreclose on houses when the owners got even the teeniest bit behind in payments. He'd turn them right out of their homes, widows or not. And that's not just idle gossip, because I know for a fact that it's true."

"Well, Miss Evangeline couldn't help what her father did. She told me that a Carver never turned away anybody who was in need. Maybe, although she felt that way, her father didn't."

Miss Ann poured more tea. "No, she couldn't help what her father did. And she's gone, so there's no use in speaking ill of the dead."

"Do you know anything about those relatives of hers or the people who work for her?" I asked.

"Not one blessed thing about the relatives and only a little about her cook, gardener, and housekeeper. And that's fine with me. Have more shortbread, Nettie. You've been looking a bit peaked lately. I don't think you're eating right."

RECIPE FOR MISS ANN'S SHORTBREAD

    1 cup of butter
    1/2 cup of brown sugar
    2 1/4 cups of flour

Mix all together until it forms a moist lump. Turn onto a floured board. Roll out to 1/4 inch thick. Cut into squares or rectangles. Bake at 375 degrees until the pieces are slightly brown around the edges.

Chapter 9

The day of Miss Evangeline's funeral dawned gray and dreary, suitable weather for the heavy feeling in my heart. It was to be a simple affair. Her family had decided she wouldn't want a big send-off. I wasn't so sure. Maybe she would have liked to go out with a splash. As it happened, though, it's doubtful that anyone at the graveside service would ever forget that day.

"What do you think about this?" I asked Ulysses, who had trudged up the stairs behind me and followed me into my bedroom.

I held up a navy blue skirt with a matching heavy sweater.

He sighed, dismissing the world of humans with their frivolous concerns, and plunked down on the rug by my bed.

"Penny?" I asked.

She didn't bother to raise her head from the pillow.

I had worn so much black lately to various funerals that I didn't want to add to the dreariness with that somber color, but navy blue wasn't much better. From what I had seen of Miss Evangeline, she wouldn't have approved of anything drab or dreary. I remembered the bright shirt she had worn the only time I saw her. No, the day was dark enough already. Hanging the skirt and sweater back in my closet, I pulled out slacks and a red sweater.

"Is this better?" I asked Ulysses.

He blinked, which I took to mean Yes.

I would go to Miss Evangeline's send-off wearing a color that celebrated her long and lively life. Besides, a raincoat would be necessary, and it would cover up most of me.

Slipping into my funeral outfit, I fluffed up my hair, applied a dab of lipstick, and declared myself fit to be seen in public.

Thunder rumbled ominously in the distance, reminding me that I had better carry an umbrella too. Why had I agonized over what to wear? Nobody at the cemetery would notice or remember what I wore. And it didn't really matter to anyone but me.

I had no invitation to Miss Evangeline's funeral. That wasn't the way things were done in small-town Ednalee. Her death notice and a short obituary were in the local paper, giving the date and time for her burial. That was enough for anyone who was interested. It was such a murky day and, according to the Tulsa meteorologist, storms were a possibility. Only those who were dedicated to the small owner of the Carver farm or the curious would dare to face the elements.

Would the murderer make an appearance? For, in my heart, I believed that Miss Evangeline's death was not accidental. Maybe, for some reason, her gentle mare was startled and pitched her off, causing her to hit her head and die. Or, maybe it was only meant to look that way. Would I see guilt on anybody's face as they stood around her coffin? I doubted that the guilty person's conscience would overcome him and he would break down and confess at her graveside, but one never knew.

At last, the hands of my old-fashioned wall clock pointed to one thirty. It was time to make the trek to the cemetery, that final resting place of past Ednalee citizens, including Uncle Javin. It always made me sad to go there and, try as I might, I couldn't feel any of the joy I had known while my uncle was here on earth. All I could feel was emptiness and the sadness that he, my last living relative, was gone.

A big green awning flapped in the wind at the cemetery. People were already gathering—the family and, I supposed, several of Miss Evangeline's employees, were sitting under the shelter of the canopy.

Others stood close by. I saw Cade and took my place beside him. His hand closed around mine, warm and comforting. I smiled at him.

The pastor of the Methodist church, Reverend Hershel Hart, began the service by reading John 14:1-4. After he sat down, to my surprise, Ken Riley stepped to the microphone. In a rich baritone, he sang the old hymn, "Day By Day." Tears filled my eyes at the lovely words.

After Ken sat down, the pastor returned and read Miss Evangeline's obituary.

The wind steadily rose, flapping the canopy with such enthusiasm that it was difficult to hear Pastor Hart's words. I glanced at Cade. He squeezed my hand. Leaning close to my ear, he said, "Maybe you'd better go home, Ned. Looks like a pretty bad storm is heading our way."

I shook my head. If he was staying, I was staying. Stubbornness is a strong character trait in my family.

Lightning flashed and the rain began, just some sprinkles at first. I heard Cade's phone when it signaled he had a text message.

"Let's stand for The Lord's Prayer," Pastor Hart said.

As everyone outside the tent was already standing, that meant only those under it rose to their feet. Before we could open our mouths to say, "Our Father," a figure clothed in a small black hat, a black coat and gloves, and, I presumed, black shoes, although I couldn't see them, jumped up from her chair under the tent, brushed Pastor Hart aside, and grabbed the microphone. Who was she? Was she one of the people I had met the day of Miss Evangeline's death? With the rain, it was difficult to see.

The wind took her hat away, and her hair streamed out in the gale, whipping against Pastor Hart as he vainly tried to calm her and regain the microphone. With her black coat flapping in the wind, she reminded me of pictures of witches I'd seen in my childhood.

She pointed her shaking finger toward the family group. I would have had no problem hearing her without the microphone. "You killed her!" she shrilled. "You killed her, and may you never have a moment's peace until you confess your heinous act. Murderers!" Who was she talking to? Evidently, it was someone in the tent.

At that moment, the ominous, throaty drone of the town's tornado siren electrified the gathering. The noise rose and fell on the gusts, a warning wail to take cover. Cade dropped my hand and sprinted to the tent.

Wrenching the microphone from the woman's hands, he said, "Listen to me! You all need to leave now." People began to scatter as he continued. "Take shelter immediately. Storm watchers have spotted a tornado heading toward Ednalee. Don't panic. Just don't lose any time in getting to safety."

Wind-driven rain nearly blinded me. All at once, Gerald was at my side.

"Miss Ned, please go by and get Coradee," he said. "You all had better go to your basement as fast as you can. Tell her I'll be okay. I've got to help Cade."

I wanted to hurry but couldn't make my legs go fast enough. Struggling against the wind, I backed my SUV out of the cemetery's parking lot and drove toward my house, my heart pounding in my ears.

The sky had become as dark as night and rain came in such torrents that driving fast was not an option. Blasts of wind rocked the Escape. It seemed like an eternity before I reached my garage, pulled inside, and started to dash up the stairs for Coradee. She met me coming down and we jumped into my front seat.

I gunned the Escape up the hill toward the carport. We both tumbled out of the car and ran into the kitchen.

"The basement," I told her, my hand on her back. "Get into the basement. I've got to find Ulysses and Penny."

Locating my pets was no problem. They appeared from somewhere in the house, pressing against my ankles. I followed Coradee down the basement stairs, the animals close behind me.

I groped for the light switch and clicked it on. Down here, the storm's roar was muffled, but the walls of the basement felt as if they shuddered. Grabbing candles and matches from a shelf, I managed to light one just as the ceiling light flickered and went out. Then, Coradee and I wrapped our arms around each other and prayed.

Chapter 10

It seemed like an eternity that Coradee, Ulysses, Penny, and I crouched in the basement listening to the wind roar overhead. At last, the noise stopped, leaving an unnatural silence in its wake.

"I'm going to peek out," I said.

Coradee shivered. "Be careful, Miss Ned. I'll come with you."

She grasped the hem of my sweater.

I grinned at her. "Coradee, if a tornado sneaks through a window and grabs me, I don't think you'll be able to hold me down with my sweater. It stretches."

She giggled, the silliness of my remark breaking the tension of the last few minutes.

Together, we climbed the basement stairs. I opened the door and peeked out. An eerie kind of half-light met my eyes. After the clamor of the storm, everything seemed unnaturally calm. No rain, no wind or thunder.

Dreading what I might see, I walked slowly to the kitchen window and peered into my yard, Coradee following close behind. A few broken tree branches lay on the ground, but the carriage house and Miss Ann's house beyond the row of pines looked unscathed by the storm.

"Thank the Lord," Coradee breathed, sinking down onto a kitchen chair.

"Yes, thank the Lord," I agreed. "Are you all right? How about a cup of hot tea?"

She smiled. "Sounds perfect. Sure, I feel great, now that I know we're alive. I'm anxious about Gerald. If he doesn't call in a minute, I'll text him. I'll walk back to the carriage house as soon as I know he's okay."

"You'll do no such thing," I told her. "You should just put your feet up and rest here for a bit. First, though, we'll have that tea. Try not to worry. The police station has a basement. I'm sure Gerald and Cade took shelter. I'll call Miss Ann and make sure she's all right."

Miss Ann answered her phone on the first ring. She was as relieved to hear my voice as I was hers. She assured me she was fine.

Coradee and I were sipping our hot tea when Cade and Gerald arrived. I hadn't even thought to lock my front door when we made our frantic scramble to safety. Cade had a key, but he often forgot to have it with him. I got up to put on the coffee pot. To my knowledge, neither Cade nor Gerald had ever tried a cup of hot tea.

Gerald pulled Coradee to her feet and hugged her. Cade put his arms around me, then took the coffee pot out of my hands.

"I'll do that," he said. "You sit down and relax."

"Are you feeling all right?" Gerald asked his wife.

Coradee laughed. "My husband is worse than an old mother hen. Yes, I'm fine. I'm just glad we're all safe."

"I heard a terrific roar," I said, sinking down onto a chair and drawing a deep breath. "Did a tornado pass overhead?"

Cade nodded. "We were lucky it didn't touch down. However, the storm carried a whole lot of rain. The low-water bridges are flooding. As soon as Gerald and I drink this coffee, we're going out to check every place where the water might be dangerous and make sure barricades are going up."

"Cade, what do you think about the woman at Miss Evangeline's funeral? Who was she? And who could she have been accusing?"

Gerald answered, "That was Lila Mae Fletcher, Miss Carver's housekeeper. My pal Jimmy Norton knows her. She has a reputation for being a little—uh—eccentric."

"I don't know who she was accusing," Cade said. "I plan to get in touch with her shortly. I need to know who she had in mind and why she feels that way."

"Miss Evangeline certainly had a funeral nobody will forget," Gerald said.

I nodded. "You're right, and I hope she knows about it."

Cade got down cups and poured coffee for Gerald and himself.

We sipped tea and coffee in silence. I relished the feeling of relief now that the storm was over. After the tension, I felt drained of all energy, and the hot drink was relaxing.

Cade cleared his throat. "Before Gerald and I leave, there's something you, Coradee, and you too, Ned, need to know. Coradee, your uncle, Moe Decker, has escaped from prison. It's entirely possible he could come back to this area and contact you."

Coradee's face flushed. "Surely, you don't think he could have killed Miss Evangeline, do you?"

Shaking his head, Cade said, "No, I don't. That's just not his style. Moe Decker is a lot of things, but I don't think he's a murderer. And you, Ned, I don't think he has any particular love for you. To his way of thinking, you are the one who put him and his brother Vermouth in jail."

Pity for Coradee vied with plain old fright. Moe Decker was a nasty, mean man, as were all the Deckers with the exception of Coradee.

Coradee wiped her eyes. "Oh, Miss Ned, I'm so sorry."

I smiled at her. "Don't worry, Coradee. I'm sure he has other things on his mind besides making trouble for me. And surely, since you are married to a policeman, he won't try to contact you."

Cade finished his coffee and stood up. "Time to go," he said to Gerald.

Gerald rose and helped Coradee to her feet. "We'll drop you off at home," he said.

I stood on tiptoe to kiss Cade's cheek. "Be careful. Hopefully, everyone in town is safe. I'll call Pat and Jackie, just to make sure they are all right."

"I've already called Mom," Gerald said. "She's fine, and she said Miss Jackie and Ron are too."

After they had left, I checked all my doors to be certain they were locked. Moe Decker would not cause me to live in fear, but it would be foolish not to realize that he was a dangerous man.

Chapter 11

Sometimes, after a trauma is over, I experience a sense of euphoria. It may be a false sensation of well-being, but it sure is nice. That good feeling lasted until I sat down on the sofa with Penny on my lap and Ulysses beside me, clicked on the TV, and heard a rundown of the storm from one of my favorite announcers on the Tulsa station, Cy Reiner.

"We can be grateful the tornado didn't touch down," he said. "The northeast part of the state was hardest hit by strong winds and floods. Officials in Ednalee, situated eighty miles northeast of Tulsa, reported severe flooding. A fatality occurred when a car was swept off a low-water bridge. As yet, the identity of the occupant of the car has not been released, pending notification of the next of kin."

"What?" I yelped, jumping up and dumping Penny onto the floor. Ulysses raised his head, his ears on the alert.

A death here in Ednalee? Why hadn't I heard of it? Cade and Gerald were busy, but I'd think they could have spared a couple of minutes to update me. Grabbing my cell phone, I punched in Cade's number.

His voice sounded weary, and I suffered a brief moment of contrition. After all, how selfish could I be, taking our chief law enforcement officer away from whatever it was he was doing in the wake of the storm?

He answered my question. "Yes, there was a drowning."

"Cy Reiner didn't give a name," I said. "Do you know who it was?"

I heard Cade's indrawn breath. "Yes, I do, Ned."

He certainly wasn't making this easy for me. I waited.

"The dead woman is Lila Mae Fletcher."

I gasped. "Miss Evangeline's housekeeper? The one who stood up at the service and accused somebody of being a murderer?"

Another deep breath. "Afraid so," he said.

My head whirled.

"How opportune. If she really knew what she was talking about, if she knew that someone under that canopy actually killed Miss Evangeline, then that person doesn't have to worry now."

Cade was silent for a moment. I could imagine him shaking his head, the crease between his eyebrows growing deeper.

"Maybe," he said.

"Cade Morris! Don't you find this suspicious? Do you think her death was truly an accident?"

"Not sure yet, Ned. As we cops are fond of saying, it's an ongoing investigation. But, whatever the outcome, I want you to let me handle it. I don't want you mixed up in this at all. So, don't put on your investigator's hat. Okay?"

Why should I not? If anything shady surrounded Miss Evangeline's death or Lila Mae's, didn't I owe it to my sense of justice to dig into it? Just a bit? It wasn't that I didn't trust Cade or the other officers. It was just that they had a tendency to be secretive and slow and I had a tendency to want answers quickly. I didn't want to make a promise I couldn't keep, so I mumbled something about hoping he'd let me know when he had anything he could share. Then, I thanked him and told him good night.

As I hung up the phone, my last bit of euphoria dissolved. Miss Evangeline's long life had, as far as I knew, been peaceful—at least, I had heard of nothing mysterious connected with her. But, as Ron said, I had been gone from Ednalee for forty years, so how was I to know? One thing was obvious—her death set something in motion, something dark and evil.

What about Moe Decker? Could he have murdered Miss Evangeline? And what about Lila? Had he added her death to his long list of thefts and intimidations? Newly escaped from jail, he surely needed money. Would he be willing to kill to rob someone? But, so far as I knew, neither of the dead women had been robbed.

Ulysses plodded over to me and laid his head on my knee. Absently, I reached down and stroked his silky ears. Ron's words and Miss Ann's evaluations stirred my memory. Ron had said the Carvers had been, at times, ruthless. Miss Ann remembered that Evangeline was a flirt, leading men on, then dumping them. Had something in the past finally caught up with folk at the Carver estate? But the ruthlessness, the flirting were all a long time ago. Judson and his daughter had gone to meet their Maker. Surely, the past was dead and buried with Miss Evangeline. Or, had those old deeds been lurking all this time, crouched and waiting, springing out of the shadows with a violence that was deadly?

Chapter 12

Sleep was hard to come by, the night of the tornado. I tossed and turned, dozing, moving in and out of restless dreams. Finally, I threw back the sheet, padded downstairs to the kitchen, and reached for the aspirin bottle. One baby aspirin, a small piece of bread, a cup of milk—these things usually quieted my frazzled nerves.

I froze, the aspirin in my hand. What was that noise? It sounded as if someone had stepped on a creaky floorboard on my front porch.

I hadn't bothered to turn on the light when I came downstairs. Nightlights in the house and the dusk-to-dawn light in the yard provided enough illumination. I tiptoed from the kitchen to the front room. Ulysses had followed me downstairs and now padded along beside me, the hair on his neck standing up.

I dropped my hand onto his head. "Shh," I whispered. "Don't bark, Ulysses."

We crept toward the window, hugging the wall. My heart was playing a tattoo against my chest as I cautiously moved the curtain and peeked out. I froze. A dark shape stood inches away, trying to pry up the window. Moe Decker? Was the intruder Moe, out for revenge?

This was too much for Ulysses. He growled and lunged toward the glass, fangs bared. With his front feet on the windowsill, he barked and snarled—a furry menace with very sharp teeth.

The person on my porch looked up. In the darkness, all I could see were two beady eyes. Was it a man or a woman? A hand flashed out, pulled a hood down over its face, then the figure whirled and jumped off the porch. A door slammed, and a dark car roared down the driveway, past the carriage house, and onto the street.

I slid down the wall, my breath coming in hard gasps. I sat on the floor, waiting for my heartbeat to return to normal. Ulysses pressed against me, licking my face.

"Oh, Ulysses," I muttered, "the best thing I ever did was adopt you."

Pushing myself up, I returned to the kitchen, my legs shaking. I poured leftover coffee into a cup, put it in the microwave for a few seconds, and, with my reheated brew, sank into a kitchen chair.

I reached for my phone, ready to punch in Cade's number, then I noticed the time. Three a.m. He'd had a hard day and, hopefully, was sleeping. The intruder hadn't made it into the house. I had seen the car speeding toward the street. Nothing would be gained by waking Cade. He had enough on his mind without worrying about a break-in that hadn't happened.

It's a strange thing with coffee—it should have jangled my already frazzled nerves, but instead, it steadied me. Anger took the place of fear. How dare someone try to break into my house? What was he after? What would he have done if he had gotten in?

"Come on, Ulysses," I said to my faithful protector. "You scared him off and we're safe."

Hurrying upstairs, I took the handgun from the drawer in my bedside table. Ulysses followed me back to the dining room, the room with the fireplace and a loveseat in front of it. Laying the gun on a side table, I huddled down on the sofa and pulled an afghan over me. My mind raced, going over and over the events of the last few days. I didn't think I'd ever feel safe enough to sleep again. I repeated Psalm 91. The Lord was with us. He would protect us.

I meant to sit there, my ears straining to catch every sound, until the sun came up, but, little by little, my taut muscles relaxed. Finally, I slid down on the cushions and sleep overtook me.

Chapter 13

Rain drumming on the porch woke me. For an instant, I wondered why I was on the love seat instead of upstairs in my bed. Then, memory flooded back and with it, a sense of bewilderment. Had someone really tried to break in, or was the whole early morning episode just another nightmare?

My mind felt foggy, and my eyes felt hot. I stood up from the love seat, stretched, and automatically went about the motions of feeding and watering my two animals, while my thoughts whirled around that dark figure on the porch. It seemed so much like a bad dream that I began to doubt whether it had happened until I saw the empty coffee cup and the aspirin bottle on the table where I had left them, visible proof that the intruder on my porch had been real.

Soon, the aroma of fresh-brewed coffee filled the kitchen. I sat down at the table with my cup of hot caffeine and tried to make sense of the last few days.

Should I tell Cade about the person on the porch this morning? If there had been any clues as to his identity, the rain would surely have washed them away. But, I couldn't rest until I checked it out myself.

I shrugged into a light jacket, grabbed a flashlight, and took Ulysses with me onto the porch. The morning sky was dark under low clouds. Rain beat against the roof and dripped off the eaves. I shone the light on the porch where the stranger had stood. My heart thudded. Several fresh scars in the paint showed where he had tried to remove the screen. The windows in this old house were long ones, reaching nearly from floor to ceiling. If he had gotten the screen off, he would have had no trouble in slipping a crowbar under the sash and prying it open. What if I hadn't come downstairs for the milk and aspirin? What if I hadn't had Ulysses with me?

Shining the beam around the porch, I saw nothing at all that did not belong there. Nothing except—I knelt down and examined a small object sticking up from between the boards. It was a flat piece of black metal rimmed with gold. A hole in one end identified it as part of a key ring. Gingerly holding it by the edges, between my thumb and forefinger, I shone the flashlight's beam onto it. A tiny gold replica of a large house was emblazoned in the center. Under it were two letters: CF. The house looked familiar. Could it be the Carver farm? That would account for the initials. Was this morning's culprit a member of the Carver family or possibly someone who worked there? Was the key ring exclusive to the estate or were they for sale somewhere?

Calling to Ulysses to follow, I went back into the house. Placing the key ring on the table, I stood staring at it. What a puzzle! And what did I have to do with any of the events of the last few days? Why would someone from the farm want to break into my house? What did I have that anyone could possibly want? I shuddered at a vile thought—did he just want to silence me? I was, after all, the person in whom Miss Evangeline had confided.

That was my only connection—Evangeline and her request. I didn't have the paper she had given me any longer—Ron had it—but I knew her wishes. Was Ken Riley the one who tried to break in? He knew I was suspicious and had made the trip to the place where she died, looking for any clues pertaining to her death. But, why would Ken care? He had wanted to know what Miss Evangeline and I discussed, but I hadn't told him.

Was the intruder Moe Decker, out for revenge? To his twisted way of thinking, it was my fault that he had been sent to jail.

After showering, I slipped into blue jeans and a red sweatshirt, ran a comb through my curls, pulled on some socks, and stepped into my brown loafers. Maybe today I could find some answers to the Carver puzzle.

As I sat at the table with my third cup of coffee, Penny purring on my lap, Ulysses under the table, and the rain falling steadily against the windows, my eyes grew heavy and my head drooped. I needed to think about Miss Evangeline's death and Lila Mae Fletcher driving into a flooded bridge crossing, but my lack of sleep was catching up with me and my thoughts were definitely muddled. My mind needed to be sharp. I had to think through this puzzle, but my body was demanding that I crawl into bed, pull the covers over my head, and forget about violence and mysteries. We humans are a paradox.

Talking aloud sometimes helps me sort things out. So, I now addressed Penny.

"I need more information," I told her. "Cade isn't telling me everything about Lila Fletcher's death. I wonder if there's something about Miss Evangeline he's keeping to himself? And who, besides Cade, could give me some answers?"

A sneeze interrupted my pondering.

"I sure hope I don't have a cold coming on," I said as Ulysses nudged my knee. "Yes, I know you need a chewy bone or a treat. You've been a good boy, and I don't blame you for not going out in this downpour. I wouldn't want you to catch a cold either."

I snapped my fingers as a thought occurred to me. "What a good idea! Thanks, Ulysses."

I would go see Dr. Ghormley. After all, maybe this sneeze meant I was catching a cold, or worse. Probably not, but a person couldn't be too careful. My aching head was not a figment of my imagination, and although I was pretty sure it was due to lack of sleep, it could be a symptom of the onset of a really bad malady. In either event, it was a good excuse to go see my doctor.

I remembered Don Ghormley from grade school, a small, skinny boy with a shock of black curls and serious brown eyes. He had grown into a tall, skinny man. He still had a head full of curls, although they were more gray than black now, and serious brown eyes. He sometimes came to services at Rose Chapel, probably when his uncertain doctor's schedule allowed it. The years had sat lightly on Don Ghormley. But, the really neat thing about him was that, as well as having a private practice, he was our county medical examiner. Surely, he had to sign the death certificates for Miss Evangeline and Lila. I wondered what he knew about these two women that I didn't know. And if he knew, would he tell me? Only one way to find out. I picked up the phone.

Don Ghormley hung his stethoscope around his neck and nodded at me as I perched on the edge of his examining table. "Ned, I'd say you are as healthy as a horse. Just get plenty of rest and drink lots of liquids."

"Thanks, Don," I said, sliding from the table and shrugging into my jacket. "You probably have a lot of people coming in with colds due to this changeable weather."

He nodded. "A few more than usual."

Sometimes, a straightforward approach is the best approach. "I understand you are our county medical examiner. With Miss Evangeline's death and that drowning last night, it's a wonder you aren't down with a cold too. Probably not getting enough rest, are you?"

He looked puzzled for a moment. "What drowning? Oh, you mean Miss Fletcher. Hmm. Business has picked up, I'm afraid. You're free to go, Ned. I'd love for you to stay so we could chat, but I've got another patient who can hardly wait to come in here and get a flu shot!"

So, Dr. Ghormley, the serious young man, was now a serious physician who wasn't about to abuse doctor-patient privilege, even if the patient was dead. I'd have to wait for Cade to tell me what I wanted to know. Which meant I'd probably wait a long time. One important thing was that Don had at first seemed puzzled when I called Lila a drowning victim. Did that mean she didn't drown, or was Dr. Ghormley simply absentminded?

Don Ghormley's receptionist wasn't any more talkative than he, but a woman in the waiting room was.

"Thanks, Mrs. McNeil," the receptionist said as she handed me a receipt for the money I had given her.

"You're welcome, Louise. The rain looks like it'll keep on all day. I hope we don't have any more flooding," I said as I turned to leave.

"Right! We don't need another drowning like that poor Lila Fletcher. Isn't it awful? First, Miss Carver's death and then her poor housekeeper," Dr. Ghormley's prospective patient, a woman in a purple sweater and tight purple pants, said, shaking her head.

"Terrible," I agreed.

"Such a pity about Miss Carver. My son's friend is an ambulance attendant. He said if Miss Carver had gotten help sooner, she might be alive today."

I stopped on my way to the door.

"Do you mean she wasn't killed instantly?" I asked.

The woman shook her head. "Nope, not according to the attendant."

I thought about this as I dashed through the rain to my car. I thought about it all the way home. So, Miss Evangeline hadn't died when her head hit the rock? How long did she remain unconscious? And then, a disturbing idea occurred to me. Was she dead when Ken found her? Surely, she was or he would have tried to get help for her.

As I drove under my carport and ran into the kitchen, I rehearsed what little I had learned before Dr. Ghormley clammed up. The only thing, actually, was that he was puzzled for a moment when I called Lila a drowning victim. So, if she didn't drown, how did she die? Then there was the woman in the waiting room. Was she right about Miss Carver being unconscious but alive for a long while before she died? Of course, Don Ghormley knew approximately how long Miss Evangeline had been dead when she was found. Medical examiners determined this as part of their job, didn't they? At least, that's what they did on those forensic shows on television. This was extremely confusing. I really needed to talk to Cade.

Chapter 14

I invited Cade to eat lunch with me after church on Sunday. When he wasn't on duty, we often went to a restaurant after leaving Rose Chapel, but I wanted him all to myself today so I could ask him some pertinent questions.

Pot roast with potatoes and gravy, corn on the cob, hot rolls, peach cobbler—these were some of Cade's favorites, and he enjoyed my cooking, if I do say so. I firmly believe that a good meal can pave the way to a man's heart and also provide a tasty way to many confidences and shared information. If guilt raised its nasty head at my little subterfuge, I quickly stuffed it back into my subconscious. The truth was, I enjoyed Cade's company.

He carried the dishes to the sink, rinsed them, and stuck them in the dishwasher while I put leftovers into the refrigerator.

"Let's take our coffee to the back porch," I suggested.

The day was sunny. Thankfully, the rain had gone somewhere else, and a clear blue sky arched overhead. I sank into a lawn chair with Cade in a chair beside me and Ulysses soaking up the sun at our feet.

Cade looked at me, quirked one eyebrow, and grinned.

"You are just bursting with curiosity, aren't you?"

I feigned innocence. "What? Me?"

He actually laughed out loud as he took my hand. "Yes, you, Miss Curiosity. Well, I have a few questions too, like, what have you learned that you haven't told me?"

I carefully peeled back the tissue paper from the key holder I had carried to the porch with me.

"Let me tell you where I found this," I said.

Cade took the key holder from me, holding it by its edges, and scrutinized it while I told him about the attempted break-in.

He scowled. "Why didn't you call me?"

"The prowler didn't get in. I saw him leave and I had Ulysses and my gun with me. Besides, you sort of had your hands full with the flood and Miss Fletcher's death. Don't be angry, Cade."

"I'm not," he said. "But remember that Moe is on the loose—haven't found him yet. If this should happen again, don't wait. Call. Okay?"

I agreed that I would.

"I'll take this to the lab guys and see if there are prints. Whether they will match any we have on file is another thing."

Maybe I wouldn't mention the visit to the pasture with Ken. Or the scuffed up area behind the cedars. Cade had, after all, lectured me about not messing with the investigation.

I told him about Dr. Ghormley's talkative patient. I hated to cast any sort of suspicion on Ken Riley. He seemed like an honest, reliable person, but I wanted to know if Miss Evangeline had died instantly or if, maybe, she was still alive when Ken found her.

"I've talked to Ken," was all he said.

"Next question—Miss Lila Fletcher. She did drown, didn't she? Or, did she die another way?"

Cade's shoulders rose and fell with a deep breath. "According to Doc Ghormley, she didn't drown. There was no water in her lungs. She wasn't wearing a seat belt—at least, she wasn't when we found her. She had some bumps and bruises. Doc said she died of strangulation, by means of something around her neck. She was wearing a heavy gold chain with a brooch. It was looped around her neck, tangled and wound tight. Was that caused by banging around inside her car when it was caught in the flood? Maybe. I suppose if she was struggling, fighting the water, she might have caught her hands in it and wrapped it tight enough to choke her, but that seems far-fetched. Or, did someone twist it—some second person in the car with her?"

I digested this bit of information in silence. She was killed by strangulation. Miss Evangeline was killed by hitting her head on a rock. She had suspected someone was trying to kill her only a short time before her death, and Lila had accused someone who was sitting under the tent of being a murderer.

"What we have is a murderer who has struck twice," I muttered.

"You may be right," Cade said. "I don't want to jump to conclusions. The forensic experts in Tulsa can tell us a lot."

"But, Miss Evangeline has already been buried," I said.

"Doc Ghormley made a thorough examination, took a lot of pictures, and is in the process of studying his results," Cade said, reaching down to ruffle Ulysses' ears.

"The M.O. is different for each one," I said. "Miss Evangeline's murder may have been thought out, but it sounds like Lila Mae was killed on impulse, with whatever was at hand."

Cade laughed. "M.O.? You are becoming quite the detective, aren't you? Would you like for me to deputize you?"

I blushed. "Somebody was listening to Miss Evangeline the night she told me about her plans for the estate," I said. "She thought she heard someone, and although I didn't see anyone, I had the feeling we were not alone. That person didn't want her to talk to Ron and make a will cutting them out of the inheritance. So, she opportunely died. Then, whoever murdered her didn't want Lila to tell anyone her suspicions, so she died too. And, Cade, I think the same person tried to break into my house. He or she, whichever, thinks I still have that paper she had me sign."

Cade regarded me silently.

"Well?" I asked. "Do you think I'm right?"

Slowly, he nodded. "You may be. But, we have no proof, Ned. You said there could have been someone listening to Miss Evangeline.

Maybe that person doesn't know for sure what all she told you. Maybe that unseen listener thinks Miss Evangeline may have named names of people she suspects."

I shuddered. "She didn't, Cade. She just said she didn't trust any of her relatives and thought somebody was trying to kill her."

He squeezed my hand. "I know that, but the killer doesn't. Unless he decides to come clean and confess, it's going to be hard to prove anything. Gerald and I are working on it. A killer always slips up somewhere. I'm talking to everybody who was at the Carver place the night Miss Evangeline died. And to a few who weren't there. I'm glad Ron has that paper you and Miss Carver signed, but the person who tried to break into your house doesn't know he has it. Killers are jittery, nervous. They suspect everybody. Or, both deaths could be accidents. That would be nice."

He leaned back against the chair and closed his eyes. "Actually, I'd like for Sunday to be a day of peace, even for law enforcement," he said. "But, there's no rest for the weary. As well as the Carver question and Miss Fletcher, a teenage gang is at work in Ednalee."

My conscience smote me. "I'm sorry, Cade. I shouldn't have brought up anything relating to crime or unsolved cases, but I had no idea little Ednalee has such big-city crime as a teen gang. What have they been doing?"

"Breaking into homes, stealing computers and anything related to technology. Also cars. A few cars have been stolen. Probably they want to sell this stuff to get money for meth or something harder."

"So, you think it could have been a teenager who tried to break into my house?"

He nodded. "Maybe. Of course, you also have that key holder, but then, if it was a kid, he could have stolen that too."

This peaceful Sunday was a direct contrast to the tangled web surrounding the Carvers. The sun shone warmly on my shoulders. A mockingbird trilled his repertoire of songs. Ulysses slept, his head on Cade's boot.

I stroked Penny, who dozed on my lap. How wonderful if the day was no more complicated than it seemed at this moment. If only greed and fear and hatred didn't exist in this world.

Cade dozed off, his face relaxed and at rest. I loved having him near. Would he ever ask me to marry him? If he did, what would my answer be? My fickle heart wasn't sure. He hadn't had a happy first marriage, as I had. His wife, Lena, left him several years before she died. Cade had a daughter who was a missionary. I had yet to meet her. Maybe some-day I would. He seemed reluctant to commit to another marriage and, truth be told, so was I. As Ron said, we all have a past. I remembered my husband Sloan and missed him greatly. How could I fully commit to Cade when the memory of Sloan took up so much of my heart?

Cade's cell phone played a snatch of "Ghost Riders." He awoke with a start, listened for a bit, and clicked it off.

"Just a reminder that I need to go see Ron Murray tomorrow. He's with a group that's interested in tracking down these young hoodlums and maybe see if we can get them into a rehabilitation program—the underage ones, that is. It's a tricky legal issue, but if we could make a judge see that rehab is a whole lot better than jail, that would be great."

"Wonderful! No wonder you're tired. Has Ron come to any conclu-sions about Miss Evangeline's lack of a will? He said that when a person dies without a will, usually the next of kin inherits. If so, shouldn't we be looking pretty closely at her family?"

"I'm doing that," he said.

"And?" I asked.

"It's an ongoing investigation, Ned," he said.

Chapter 15

My friend and part-time employer Daisy Stanton didn't think much of my great idea. She tucked a wisp of hair behind her ear and shook her head.

"No, that wouldn't be good, Ned. I appreciate the fact that you want to get into the Carver house to talk to those people and see what's going on since Miss Evangeline's death, but I don't like involving the real estate company. It's too much like being an ambulance chaser."

She picked up her cup of coffee and stared unblinkingly at me over its rim.

A niggling conscience prompted me to voice what was on my mind. "Do you mean it sounds like I'd be taking advantage of Miss Evangeline's death to drum up business for your real estate firm if I just took an innocent little trip out there to find out if they plan to sell the farm?" I asked, toying with my cup of coffee.

"That's what I mean. Now, when all the dust settles, if somebody is goofy enough to sell that wonderful piece of property, believe me, I'd love to be the one to handle it. But, we don't know that will happen. I don't think Miss Carver's will has even been probated or read, has it?"

I sighed. "No. She didn't have one."

Daisy Stanton was a new friend. I had connected with her through the Old Houses Club. Librarian Greta Thatcher had introduced me to that group. At the first meeting I attended, Daisy asked me if I'd like a job taking pictures of old houses in Ednalee for her advertisements in the paper and a sales brochure. Of course, I jumped at the chance to see the interior of some of the town's historic places, so now I had a part-time and fascinating job. But, Daisy was as scrupulous as she could be and was not enthusiastic about my idea for getting back inside the Carver house.

Grandy's was busier than usual this morning. Evidently, many people had the same idea Daisy and I had. The small coffee shop was the perfect place for a cozy chat and a cup of excellent coffee, especially when a noisy spring storm rattled the windows and made outdoor activities impossible.

Gazing at sheets of rain sliding down the windows, I said, "I need to talk to the Carver kin. I'd like them to know that I don't have that paper Miss Evangeline had me sign and maybe kind of hint that she didn't tell me much. I don't want anyone to think I know some deep, dark secret."

I smiled at Janey as she came to top off our cups with fresh coffee.

"This is kind of like shooting in the dark—I don't know if the person who tried to get into my house was a Carver, and I don't know if that paper was what he was after. But, if it was, then I'd feel safer if they all knew they can stop trying to get it from me. Ron has it."

Daisy shook her head. "Tell me again about that paper."

Even though I had told Miss Evangeline I would keep her wishes to myself, I figured with her death, that promise was null. Besides, it seemed important to explain why somebody might have had a motive for murder. So, I repeated the story of Miss Evangeline's plans to leave her home to the state.

"The duplicate that Miss Carver and you signed has probably been destroyed by this time," Daisy mused, stirring her coffee.

I snapped my fingers. "I've just thought of something."

Daisy jumped. "What?"

"Greta! Greta could have another Old Houses Club luncheon and invite the women from the farm. There's Myra, she's the cook, and Pearly, and Veda. Then they would all be together, nobody would be suspicious, and I could tell them I don't have that document and am not interested in what's going to happen to Miss Evangeline's estate."

This would be true, in a way. What I was interested in was bringing a killer to justice, if a killer existed.

As chairwoman of the club that studied the history of Ednalee's houses, Greta should be the one to extend an invitation. We had a luncheon in a member's home once a month.

Daisy motioned to Janey. "Would you bring a doughnut, please?" she asked when Janey appeared at our table.

"I'm going to need a sugar boost to follow all this," she said. "I wish you would tamp down that curiosity of yours, Ned."

With her cup full and her doughnut in front of her, Daisy said, "So, you are going to just casually announce to everyone assembled at the luncheon that you don't have that signed paper?"

"Sure," I said, enthusiasm beginning to edge its way into my thoughts. "Why wouldn't that work?"

Daisy was silent for a moment. "I guess it could, but it's going to be kind of tricky to find an opening to blurt out something like that."

I shook my head. "Well, then, I won't blurt it out. I'll just mention it to each Carver relative, one at a time, as if I'm sharing a confidence."

Daisy grinned. "Ned, you have certainly livened up this old town. I guess you can't help it if you're involved in every suspicious death that happens. But, sometimes meddling is risky business."

Meddling? I was sure Daisy meant to say *investigating*.

I sniffed. "Daisy, I'm amazed at you. I am not meddling. It was through no fault of my own that I've become involved."

Daisy swallowed a dainty sip of coffee and dabbed her mouth with her napkin.

"It will probably be good to invite the women to the OHC luncheon, hope they come, whisper in their little ears that Ron has the paper, and then, let them know that you think Miss Evangeline was just senile and you didn't take what she said seriously. But, if they actually know nothing of Miss Evangeline's plan, you'll be stirring up a hornet's nest."

I realized that. Miss Evangeline's death could have been accidental. Miss Fletcher may have died due to her car being swept off a bridge, and the person trying to get into my home was, maybe, a vagrant or a juvenile delinquent out to rob me of valuables. But, what about the keyholder? What about the insignia *CF?*

I rested my elbows on the table and cupped my hands around my face. "My head hurts. Do you have an aspirin?"

Daisy searched her purse for the little headache reliever, handed me a tablet, and said, "I don't blame you, Ned, for being upset. And I know you are trying your best to think this thing through, but just be sure you don't say or do anything that will make matters worse, okay? If your suspicions are correct, the murderer will not want you interfering with his plans. Your life could be in danger. I'd sure hate to lose a good employee."

"Believe me," I said, "I don't want that either."

Chapter 16

The thunderstorm had slowed to a nice, gentle rain by the time Daisy and I left Grandy's. I drove to the city library, parked in the lot, and, holding my umbrella over my head, hurried up the library steps. I left my umbrella on the porch.

Greta was busily sorting through books behind the front desk. She looked up and smiled as I came in.

"Come join the party," she said. "I think this rain has put a stop to outdoor activities. Everyone in Ednalee must be here today."

"No," I said. "Only half is here. The other half is at Grandy's."

How much should I tell Greta? If she knew of my involvement in Miss Evangeline's death, she would only worry, and enough of my friends were concerned as it was. I certainly would not lie, but I'd see if I could figure out a believable reason for my request.

"It's almost time for another meeting of the Old Houses Club, isn't it?" I asked, squelching a feeling of guilt for not telling Greta my reason for mentioning this.

"Sure is. I'm having it at my house this time. It should be a fun time. Miss Ann is going to read to us from a journal that belonged to her mother. It tells about the first houses built here in town."

"What a treat. She didn't say a word about it to me," I said, trying to think of a way to voice my suggestion. As it turned out, Greta provided the opening for me.

"I think we need some new blood in the group. We've lost two of our members, and I certainly don't want to discontinue the meetings."

"Nor do I," I agreed. "I've thought of a few others who might enjoy coming. As you know, Miss Evangeline Carver passed away recently, and I'm sure those at her home are feeling her loss. Do you think it's too soon to invite the ladies from the Carver estate?"

Greta blinked. "No," she said slowly, "I don't suppose that would be insensitive. I don't know any of them. Of course, my husband's cousin Jules works out there, but I haven't even talked to him for quite a while."

"Jules? Do you mean the gardener?"

"That's the one. Jules Thatcher." She sighed. "I've never understood why he wanted to work there, after the way his father was treated by Judson Carver years and years ago."

I was beginning to be glad I had dropped into the library. Why hadn't I thought of Greta sooner?

Leaning across the desk, I asked, "What did Judson Carver do years ago?"

"It's no secret, Ned, even though I don't want gossip to start again. Sometimes libraries seem to have ears." She nodded across the room to a man reading a book of bound papers. His back was toward me, but the set of his head looked familiar.

"That's Ken Riley," Greta said. "He works at the Carver farm. He has been in twice lately and looked through copies of some old newspapers, papers from out of state. Not sure what's so interesting in them. Maybe he's a historian."

"Sure," I whispered. "I've met Ken. He seems like a nice enough person."

"I guess I just suspect everyone who has anything to do with the Carvers," she said. "Many years ago, the Thatcher family lost their home due to Judson Carver foreclosing on it. Jules was only a little boy at the time, but, of course, he knew the story. Shortly after Jules's father lost the home, he died. Jules's mother had a terrible time trying to make ends meet. Judson Carver didn't lift a finger to help, just sold the house and tucked more money into his family's coffer."

"That's awful," I said, blinking away tears. "Ron Murray said that Judson was ruthless."

Greta nodded. "That's the word."

Shrugging her shoulders, she said, "That was a long time ago, and yes, I'll invite the Carver women. What are their names? And why should they want to come? This is kind of an out-of-the-blue invitation, Ned."

I stared down at Greta's desk, drumming my fingers on its smooth surface. I really hadn't thought this out very well. In fact, I hadn't thought it out at all. I was getting a lot of practice today in thinking on my feet.

"Tell them—tell them that we're going to have a terrific program. First, Miss Ann will speak, and then I am going to add to it with a short talk called 'If Walls Had Ears.' Say that I've been investigating some murder mysteries in our county and I may have an important announcement."

Greta frowned and shook her head.

"Since you haven't met the people who live there now, I'll invite them," I said. "How's that? I could go to the house, express my condolences on the recent deaths, and ask if they're up to a luncheon. Sort of give them something positive to think about."

"To make it more official, and not look like you're being nosy, I'll print out an invitation for you to take along," Greta said. "I'll have it ready tomorrow if you want to drop by and pick it up before you go to the Carvers'."

"Thanks! I should offer my sympathy anyway. After all, that family has suffered a lot of loss in a short time. It'll be good for them to get their minds onto something else for a bit."

Greta folded her arms across her chest and frowned at me. "Ned McNeil, I don't know what you've got up your sleeve, but I sure hope you know what you're doing. You are getting a reputation, you know, for being involved in police matters, and you are downright devious at times."

I wanted to leave before Ken turned around and saw me. "Greta, I'm surprised at you! In no way am I devious, and I always know what I'm doing."

As well as being stubborn, I believe in the power of positive thinking.

Chapter 17

Jackie invited Pat and me to her house for lunch. This was a good sign, maybe an indication that whatever crisis she faced had passed, or maybe she was simply ready to share her problem. I put off my visit to the Carver place until that afternoon.

The salad and sandwiches were delicious. We sat at Jackie's round dining table, sunlight streaming through sheer yellow curtains, and enjoyed a brownie with coffee.

Gazing at her cup, Jackie sighed and spoke without looking at us.

"I'd like to talk about something, if you don't mind. I know you two can keep this under your hats."

"The Three Musketeers," Pat murmured. "One for all, and all for one."

"It's Ron," Jackie said. "Or, maybe it's me. I don't know. He's been working late, missing supper many times, and he seems to have just lost interest in me. I was afraid he had found somebody else, somebody exciting and younger."

Holding my breath, I waited for Jackie to go on. Ron? I had seen the devotion these two had for each other, and it was hard to believe that Ron didn't love Jackie as much as he ever did.

Jackie sighed. "Finally, last night we had a long, heart-to-heart talk. He assured me that all was well as far as his affections went, but he thought I had become distant, uninterested in him. Can you believe it? Why should he think that?"

Pat's face was a study—raised eyebrows, lips pressed together.

Shaking her head, Jackie went on. "Turns out, it's his job. Now how do I compete with a law practice he loves and knows like the back of his hand?"

I felt a sense of relief at Jackie's news. Their marriage might have a few cracks in it, but surely it wasn't broken past repair.

"He has been a lawyer here in town for many years," Pat said. "Why is it suddenly becoming a problem?"

Jackie got up to refill our coffee cups. "He's taken on too much work. He's involved with a civic group in town that's trying to help teens and preteens before they're entangled in the justice system—kids who are headed down the wrong road and need guidance. He's so passionate about it, and I think it's consuming his every waking thought."

"That isn't a bad thing," I said. "Cade mentioned that some teens in town are becoming a menace, breaking into houses and stealing cars. If they can be turned around, that will be wonderful. Is that what you're talking about?"

Jackie nodded. "Yes. There's one boy in particular, barely twelve years old. He and his older brother, who's eighteen, live alone since their dad died. Ron thinks the older brother is pretty rotten and, although there's no proof of it, Ron's afraid he's leading the younger one, Mike, down the wrong road."

"Ron just can't say no when someone needs help," Pat said, raising her cup to her lips. "He's certainly available for Gerald when my son has a question about a law course from the university."

"I don't begrudge his time spent with Gerald," Jackie said, "but that brings up something else, Pat, which isn't your fault at all, and I shouldn't even mention it."

Pat and I waited.

"With Coradee and Gerald being prospective parents, I think it brings our childlessness back to Ron in a big way. He would have liked to have children, way back when we were first married, and I would have too, but it just didn't happen. We talked about adopting, but, well, one thing led to another—his busy law practice, my teaching job—and we sort of put it behind us."

Thinking of all the children who needed loving parents, I felt a little surprised at my friend.

The sunny dining room fell silent except for the soft click of our cups on coasters.

Drawing a deep breath, Jackie said, "Well, you're right. Adoption should have been top priority. Ron and I both love children, but I had my kindergartners, and I guess I was selfish in not considering Ron's wishes."

"You know," I said, "we can all look back and wish we had or hadn't done certain things. Decisions of the past can't be changed, but it would be sad to let those decisions disrupt your happiness right now, in the present."

A small smile quirked Jackie's mouth. "Thanks, Ned. You're right, of course. I knew I could count on both of you. You're so wise."

I laughed out loud. "That's the first time in my life anyone has called me wise. I really thought you knew me better than that."

Pat giggled. "Jackie may not, but I sure do. Your main character trait is curiosity, Ned. But then, you're pretty nice too."

On that lighter note, our luncheon broke up. Pat and I had ridden to Jackie's together. Jackie hugged us both, and as we left, I felt much better about one problem at least. Now all that was left were two deaths, in my mind suspicious deaths, and, as Pat said, I was definitely curious about both of them.

Chapter 18

For the third time, I stood at the charcoal gray door of the Carver mansion and knocked. The door opened a crack and Veda Johnson's sharp face glared at me.

"You again! What do you want?"

Determined to ignore rudeness and overcome it with grace, I smiled. "Hello there, Miss Johnson. I've come to offer my condolences for the two losses in your family. May I come in?"

"Thank you, but we're awfully busy right now." Veda was in the process of closing the door when a new voice stopped her.

"Wait! Is that any way to treat company? Do come in, Mrs. McNeil."

Pearly walked up beside Veda, a smile on her face and her hand outstretched.

Smiling in return, I stepped inside. Everything looked as it had the first time I was here—chandelier, wide plank flooring, lovely wallpaper—but I didn't feel the warmth I had felt from Miss Evangeline. Indeed, the house seemed strangely dark and empty.

"I'm really sorry about Miss Evangeline and Lila Fletcher. Two losses in such a short time! I hope you are managing to cope," I said.

"So nice of you to drop in," Pearly said. "Do you have time for a glass of tea?"

Encouraged by her friendliness, I nodded.

"Of course, if it isn't too much trouble."

Pearly motioned me down the hall. "None at all. Come on into the kitchen. It's a little homier than that huge dining room."

Veda followed Pearly as we three traipsed down the hall.

No need for the overhead light this afternoon. Sunlight streamed through the kitchen windows, brightening the room. Once again, I was amazed at the tasteful blending of the past with the present in the kitchen's furnishings. Veda and I sat at the table while Pearly brought glasses of tea.

Myra stopped peeling potatoes at the sink, turned, and stared at me.

"How are you, Myra?" I asked.

"All right. Should I leave you three alone?"

She turned to leave the room, but I stopped her. "No, please don't go, Myra. I have an invitation which includes you too."

I had all three women for an audience now. Could I say something that would let them know I didn't have Miss Evangeline's written wishes? Could I hint that I thought she was old and paranoid? Somehow, I couldn't think of the words or an opening to inject such an off-the-wall statement. No, I should wait until the luncheon to do this.

I pulled the invitation Greta had printed from my purse and handed it to Pearly.

"You may not have heard about the Old Houses Club that meets each month in town. As a spokesperson for Greta Thatcher, our president, I'd like to extend an invitation to our next luncheon. I hope it isn't too soon after the losses you've suffered. I thought perhaps it would help to take your minds away from grief, if only for an hour or so."

Veda sniffed. "Luncheon? I don't think we should be thinking of anything so frivolous, not when our hearts are heavy. Why, I cry myself to sleep every night just thinking about dear cousin Evangeline."

"To be sure," Pearly murmured, staring at the invitation.

Stillness hung heavily in this sunny room.

Pearly read the card, Veda peering over her shoulder. Wordlessly, she handed it to Myra.

To break the silence, I said brightly, "So, are you all staying here in the house now?"

Pearly's smile had been replaced by a thoughtful look. "Certainly. We felt it our duty to move in here and keep an eye on things. That's what cousin Evangeline would have wanted us to do."

"I'm not staying here at night," Myra said. "This old place gives me the creeps after dark. Besides, I have my own house to go home to each night."

"Well, you are invited too," I chirruped. "Of course, the luncheon is only for the ladies. I hope Elbert won't feel left out. Is he around somewhere?"

Sometimes my brashness amazed even me. I expected to be told it was none of my business, and Veda may have been about to do just that, but Pearly interrupted her.

"Of course. You wouldn't expect my husband to be living in the guest house, would you? Just what is supposed to happen at this luncheon, Mrs. McNeil?"

"Please, call me Ned. And, if it's all right, I'll call you Pearly. It's an interesting program. One of our octogenarians, Ann Decker, will speak about the early settlers of Ednalee and the homes they built. I love delving into history, and I've found some interesting things about the people in this town. Old-timers kept a lot of things close to the vest. It's such fun uncovering secrets, don't you agree?"

For the first time, Veda smiled. "Oh, yes. Fun."

"If you don't mind, I'll go back to peeling these potatoes, Miss Ned. Will your brother be here for lunch, Pearly?" asked Myra.

Someone else on the estate? I remembered what Miss Evangeline had said about her family gathering in like vultures.

Pearly's attitude turned frosty as she got up from her chair. "Of course, Myra. Peel enough potatoes for everyone. I'll think about your invitation, Ned. Personally, I feel it's a little soon after all this upheaval and sadness, but I'll think about it."

I arose too. Veda remained seated, still smiling.

"You can count me in," Myra called as I started out of the kitchen with Pearly. "I wouldn't miss it for the world."

Chapter 19

After Pearly closed the door behind me, I stood on the lowest step, drinking in the beauty of my surroundings. Under the warm sunshine, the buds on some of the azaleas were about to blossom. After the recent rains, all of nature smelled fresh and new, as if nothing dark or deadly had ever touched the estate.

As I started down the walk to my car, a movement in one of the flower gardens caught my attention. Glimpsing a straw hat and the back of a green shirt, I took a few steps in that direction. A man was seated on a low stool near the ground, busily clipping the bottom branches of the arborvitae that edged the garden. Could this be Jules, the gardener and Greta's husband's cousin? I'd like to meet him.

"Forgive me for interrupting your work, but I'm Ned McNeil. I know your cousin Greta," I said.

The man jumped and fell off his stool onto his backside. He scrambled to his feet, his face flaming. His round eyes and open mouth were so comical, I couldn't smother a laugh.

"Ah! Sure and 'tis givin' me a right start, you are," he said in a lilting voice straight from the Emerald Isle.

Had I stumbled onto an Irish leprechaun? For he surely looked the part. He was small, not quite as tall as I. The fringe of hair I saw below his hat was black and curly, and his eyes were as green as the bush he was trimming.

"I'm so sorry," I said, smiling in reassurance. "I came to the house to deliver a message to the women inside, and when I saw you working, I thought I'd say hello. If you are related to Greta Thatcher, let me say that she and I are friends. She told me you work for the Carvers, if your name is Jules."

Even to my own ears, my introduction sounded disjointed. Greta hadn't mentioned that her relative was Irish. I found myself copying his brogue, and had no idea why I did so. Maybe it was my reaction to his resemblance to a leprechaun and his sudden fall to the ground.

"I was here the night Miss Evangeline's body was discovered," I went on. "Let me express my condolences to you too. Have you worked in the Carver gardens long?"

He nodded. "Thank 'e. Yes, I've worked here a right smart while. And yes, Jules is my name. 'Course, I don't know what'll happen to my job now that Miss Evangeline's gone. I may soon be out of work. That Elbert person may inherit, but who's to say? I just know this old place is not the same with her gone. And I miss her. That, I do."

"Yes," I said. "Sure, and I didn't know her but a short while and I miss her too."

"What can I do for you, Miz McNeil?"

"I'm Ned, not Mrs. McNeil. As well as saying how sorry I am that Miss Evangeline is gone, I brought an invitation to a luncheon from Greta. I'm not sure the ladies in the house are coming, though."

He laughed. "I think each one is afraid to leave the estate, afraid the others might lock the door behind them and not let them back in. I've never seen so many kinfolk in one place. You'd think they'd love being together and sort of comfort each other in their grief, but I don't think they like each other very much."

So Jules was a talker.

"They don't like each other?" I echoed.

He shook his head. "I don't blame them. Elbert, he's not fit for much, and that newcomer Mick Morrow—claims he's Pearly's brother—well, I've never seen such a shifty-eyed character. Don't know what he's doing here. Pearly said he came to be with her in her hour of grief. Ha!

The only thing she's grievin' is she's afraid she might have to move now that she can't mooch off Miss Eva anymore.

"Forgive my manners, lassie. Here, sit." He scooted his gardening stool toward me. "I'll just hunker down here. May be best if nobody in the big house sees us talkin'."

Agreeing that it might be best, although I couldn't quite say why, I sat down.

"You sound as if you know Pearly and her husband pretty well," I said.

He grinned, his teeth flashing and a dimple coming and going in his cheek.

"I've got ways of finding out things," he said, pointing to his head. "Sometimes I hear conversations I'm not supposed to hear."

I feigned surprise. "Jules! You don't mean you eavesdrop?"

"You can call it what you like, miss. People shouldn't shout at each other when they're angry—not if they don't want the whole world to know what they're talkin' about. It's not hard to hear. Probably the whole county can hear when Pearly and Elbert are goin' at it.

"So, yes, I know this lot, but Miss Evangeline and I were friends," he said, his voice tinged with sadness. "Sometimes she'd get lonely. She always had a nightcap before she went to bed—a glass of wine to settle her stomach. On the times I was working late in the gardens, she'd ask me to come inside the house and join her in a drink. We'd sometimes share confidences."

Now I was getting somewhere. Jules and Miss Evangeline often had a quiet chat over a glass of wine. Maybe she told him more about the person she feared was trying to kill her.

"Say there, old man, aren't you supposed to be working?"

I jumped up and whirled around. A stranger, a tall man with shiny dark hair and eyes that matched it, stood with folded arms, frowning down at us.

"Don't blame Jules," I said. "I came to visit the women in the house and happened to see him working. So, I came over to get acquainted. I don't believe we've met."

"This is Mick Morrow," Jules mumbled.

Mick simply glared at me. It wasn't often I came up against such bare-faced hostility. I dismissed him with what I hoped was a frosty glance and spoke to Jules.

"It was nice to meet you," I said. "I'll tell Greta that you will drop in to see her soon."

With that, I turned on my heel and stalked to my car.

Chapter 20

I fumed all the way home, thinking of things I should have said and would have said if I had thought of them in time. My hindsight is good, but that rude man had caught me off guard, and I guess the shock of it sort of numbed my brain.

Ulysses and Penny met me at the door to the kitchen. I dropped to my knees and hugged Ulysses. Penny didn't go in for hugging, but I stroked her as she rubbed against my legs.

"You guys are balm for a sore ego," I told them. "You're very nice to come home to, and I think you deserve a treat."

I felt blessed that both Ulysses and Penny resided under my roof. Without them, I'd be lonely and have no one to talk to.

I made sure their food and water dishes were full, then offered each one a small snack. I was just about to fix myself a nice, calming cup of chamomile tea when the phone rang.

Caller ID told me Ken Riley was on the line. What a surprise. He sounded urgent. "Ned, are you busy tonight?" he asked.

"I just have a date with the television," I answered.

"Would you consider coming to supper with me? I really need to talk to you. The Wildwood has pretty good food. Are you interested?"

He needed to talk to me? Why on earth should he? I tried to digest this surprising statement. The Wildwood Restaurant served delicious food in a lovely atmosphere of candlelight, soft music, and a view of the river. But, why go there? What was wrong with Grandy's?

My curiosity was definitely piqued. "Sure," I said.

"I'll pick you up at six," Ken said and hung up.

"Now what was that all about?" I asked Ulysses. It couldn't be that Ken was romantically attracted to me. He was several years younger, and we had barely met. However, I admitted, there was something about him that seemed comfortable, as if I had known him for a long time.

I climbed the stairs and searched my closet for something to wear—something suitable for the Wildwood. At last I decided on a soft blue dress that draped nicely and a pair of matching low-heeled pumps.

It had been the kind of day that set the adrenaline flowing, and the run-in with the rude stranger who accosted Jules and me had really got my blood boiling. Now it all seemed to evaporate, and I realized I was tired. The bed looked inviting. Lying down for a short rest was definitely in order.

I hadn't meant to doze, but soon I was dreaming. I was riding Miss Evangeline's little mare toward the edge of a cliff. Somebody somewhere was banging a drum and shouting my name. The banging got louder, and I swam up through layers of sleep to realize the noise I heard was someone pounding on my front door.

Stumbling downstairs, yawning as I went, I heard Cade on the porch.

"Ned! Are you in there?"

He was fumbling in his jeans pocket for his key when I opened the door.

"Are you all right?" he asked. "I was about to get alarmed."

I rubbed my eyes. "Sorry. I was asleep and it took a while to hear you. Is everything all right?"

"Yes. I was just on my way home and wanted to drop in for a minute. Are you busy tonight? I'm in the mood for a hamburger and a shake from Grandy's. How about you?"

My heart plummeted. I hadn't planned on telling Cade about my dinner date with Ken. But, honesty is usually the best policy, so I took a deep breath.

Looking up into his eyes, I said all in a rush, "I'd love to, Cade, but Ken Riley asked me to eat with him at The Wildwood."

Those eyes which had been warm a second ago now reminded me of blue ice.

"Ken Riley?" he repeated.

I nodded.

"Why?" he asked.

"Well, he asked me and said he needed to talk to me, and I thought maybe he would tell me something that would shed some light on Miss Evangeline's death or, perhaps, Lila Fletcher's."

Cade's voice was quiet. "Ned, Ken Riley is a suspect in the murder of Miss Evangeline."

I felt my scalp tighten. "Murder? Do you mean Dr. Ghormley decided it wasn't an accident?"

"Her head wound—it was made with something heavy and round, but her death wasn't caused by falling on a rock. She landed on her face when she fell—the bruises and scratches testified to that. While she was lying there on the ground, someone came up, stood over her, and smashed in her head. But, when we reached her, she was lying on her back."

I felt cold all over. "How do you know this?" I whispered.

"The forensics team and Don Ghormley are pretty knowledgeable and thorough. And the doc said she was unconscious for several hours before she was found. Who found her? Ken Riley. Tomorrow I plan to bring him in for questioning."

I took Cade's hand and drew him into the house.

"Wait. Come in and sit down. I can't quite believe all this."

We went through the living and dining rooms to the kitchen. I dropped into a chair, propped my chin on my hands, and stared at Cade, sitting across from me.

"I'm sorry to be so blunt, Ned," he said, "and I wouldn't have broken it to you like this, but you said you plan to go out with this guy."

"No, I don't," I muttered. "I plan to eat supper with him and hear what he wants to say. Maybe he has news about Miss Evangeline. Maybe he found out who really killed her."

Cade's laugh was grim. "Right. And maybe he's just trying to get you on his side, or maybe he thinks you're getting to be too nosy for your own good."

"You've already convicted him in your mind, Cade. I'd like to hear his viewpoint. There could be a very good explanation for those forensic findings. It's just hard to believe Ken would kill anybody, especially Miss Evangeline. He seemed genuinely fond of her."

Cade stared at me, shaking his head. At last, he said, "So you are determined to go eat with him?"

"If you forbid me, I'll not go, but I think I should."

He left soon after. Waiting until he had disappeared down the driveway, I went to my telephone. I did not want Ken to pick me up. I'd drive and meet him at the restaurant. Being with him with others around was all right, but being alone with him in a car wasn't. Not now. Not after the bombshell Cade had just delivered. Besides, meeting him would seem less like an actual date.

Chapter 21

The host, a youngish man with a friendly smile, met me at the door of The Wildwood.

"Mrs. McNeil?" he asked. "I recognize you from the description Mr. Riley gave. Follow me. He's waiting for you."

Ken rose as I approached the table. Tonight, he wore a blue button-down-the-front shirt, western jeans that snugly fit his slim build, and expensive-looking cowboy boots.

I smiled as I sat down. "We match," I said, motioning from my blue dress to his shirt.

"You know what they say about great minds," he answered. "You look really nice, Miss Ned."

"You can drop the 'Miss,' Ken. It's good to see you under more pleasant circumstances this time."

"Yes, that's for sure. Let's order, then I'd like to talk to you about what's probably uppermost on both our minds. I trust you, out of all the people involved in Miss Evangeline's passing, and I know you'd like to see justice done. You see, I have a small confession to make, and I want you to know what I'm going to do about it."

He motioned to the waiter who suggested a house specialty, a lettuce, tomato, and cucumber salad, to get us started.

Confession? This sounded ominous. Ken looked as if he hadn't been sleeping well. His cheeks were hollow, and maybe it was the dim lighting, but he seemed pale.

Glancing around the room, I wondered if Cade was one of the diners. I had not a doubt that he was keeping an eye on me. He agreed much too easily to my meeting Ken, who he considered a suspect. Or, maybe he wasn't a diner but was hiding behind a potted plant. The thought caused me to giggle.

"Have I missed a joke?" Ken asked. "Sorry if I haven't been listening."

"No," I said, gazing appreciatively at the salad the waiter set before me. "I didn't say anything funny. I was just thinking."

"I'm glad one of us is in a good mood," Ken said.

After the salad, Ken ordered tenderloin tips and I decided on chicken. The hot rolls were homemade, feathery light and buttery. The coffee was fresh-ground. I found myself enjoying the meal a lot.

Ken was an interesting conversationalist, keeping me amused with stories of Miss Evangeline's horses and their different personalities.

"They are just like humans," he said. "Some mornings something has ticked them off and they're grouchy. Some days, they are just full of fun and devilish tricks. I can tell their moods by looking into their eyes and watching their ears."

I swallowed a bit of food. "Watching their ears?"

"Yes. Ears pricked forward are a sign of fair weather, so to speak. One ear forward and one ear back is a warning sign, and two ears laid back, well, forget about riding a horse who looks like that."

"You know so much about horses," I said. "I'm curious—how did you come to be working at Carver Farms? Are you a native of Ednalee?"

He shook his head. "No. I'm from Kentucky, actually. My mom and Miss Evangeline were friends when they were girls. Mom fell in love with a Kentucky boy who had racing in his blood, so that's how I came to be out there. I had a great childhood. We had horses on our farm, and I learned a lot from my dad. Then, Dad died, and Mom and I moved into town. Mom, I'm sorry to say, has Alzheimer's now and is in a facility for Alzheimer patients. We didn't have a lot of money while I was growing up, but there was always enough. She managed to send me to the university. When I graduated, I was sort of at loose ends—didn't know what I wanted to do. Miss Evangeline phoned Mom, asked her if I'd be interested in a job helping with her horses, and here I am."

An interesting story. So, even though Judson Carver was a tough old man, foreclosing on widows, his daughter had a soft spot for helping people—those relatives who had shown up, penniless, as well as the son of her friend. Miss Evangeline could have turned a blind eye, but she didn't. This was a good sign, reinforcing my instinctive liking for her.

Ken motioned for the waiter to refill our coffee cups.

"Miss—um, Ned, I haven't been exactly honest with you. I need to talk about the night I found Miss Evangeline."

A small prickle began at the base of my neck. I took a sip of coffee and waited for him to continue.

"I found Miss Evangeline, just like I told you. From the way the ground was torn up, I knew that Melanie had probably bucked her off and she fell on those rocks, but there's something else."

My mouth went dry.

"She was on her face when I found her and she . . . well, Ned, she was breathing. Not much, but she was still barely alive. The back of her head was all bloody and hurt. The back of it, Ned, not the front. I knelt down beside her, calling her name, and, as gently as I could, I turned her over."

My breath caught in my throat. Tears burned my eyes. "Ken, she was alive? Why didn't you call for help?"

He shook his head. "There wasn't time. She opened her eyes and looked at me. I took her hand and she said . . . she said . . ."

I held my breath while he swallowed and wiped tears from his eyes.

"She said, 'I'm sorry' and then closed her eyes, took one long breath, and she was gone. I sat with her until I knew for sure she was dead. Then, I came and told you all. I was afraid to say anything at first, afraid I'd be considered a suspect. That's the truth. I wanted you to hear it from me 'cause I'm pretty sure the sheriff and Cade Morris and Doc Ghormley have figured out a few things. I know it looks bad for me."

"Oh, Ken," I said, "why didn't you tell the sheriff right away? Because you didn't say anything and you were the one who found her, it makes you look guilty."

"But, why would I kill anybody as nice as Miss Evangeline? I swear to you, Ned, that I didn't kill her. Somebody did, and I intend to find out who. But, it wasn't me."

Chapter 22

"So, let me tell you what he said." I was talking to Ulysses about my dinner with Ken last night. I had tried to call Cade this morning, but he didn't answer. Surprising! I thought he would want to know about that revealing conversation. He wouldn't need to check on my safety. I was sure he had been somewhere just out of sight until I left the restaurant and got safely back home.

Ulysses wandered away while I was in mid-sentence. I sighed, got up from the kitchen chair, and thought about what to do next.

"When in doubt, call a lawyer," I said to nobody in particular. I would call Ron Murray. I wanted to know if he had reached a decision about Miss Evangeline's paper that I had given him. And I was interested to hear if any of her relatives had as yet contacted him.

As I reached for the phone, it rang. It was Cade.

"Ned, did Ken tell you anything about his plans last night? Did he say that he was going to leave town?" Cade asked, his voice taut.

"No," I said. "He mentioned finding Miss Evangeline and said that she was still alive when he found her, but died shortly after. He stayed with her until she breathed her last."

"Yeah. Well. That's really no surprise." I didn't often hear sarcasm in Cade's voice, but I heard it now.

"Last night, one of my guys tailed him until he left the city limits," Cade said. "A sheriff's deputy was supposed to follow him then, but the guy lost him. He's not home this morning. Truck is gone. Nobody at the farm knows where he is. Looks like he's flown the coop. Now are you convinced he's guilty? An innocent person wouldn't run away."

"No, I'm not convinced. I agree that it was a dumb thing for him to do, but he said he was going to find out who killed Miss Evangeline. Maybe he's following up on some sort of hunch. Besides, what reason would he have to murder a boss who, evidently, was good to him? His mom in Kentucky and Miss Evangeline were friends."

"I've got an idea or two on that," Cade said. "Meanwhile, if he contacts you or you hear of him, will you give me a call?"

"You know I will," I answered.

This was a surprising development. Ken had not acted wisely about the whole episode of finding Miss Evangeline. Certainly, he should have told Cade she was alive when he reached her and what she said to him. I don't know why she said those two words, *I'm sorry*. They didn't make sense to me, but maybe she thought they would to Ken. Leaving town made Ken a fugitive, even if he wasn't guilty.

I made the appointment with Ron and started to his office early enough to drop by the library and talk to Greta.

"So, you think those gals at the farm might actually come to the luncheon?" Greta asked.

I shrugged. "They're thinking about it. Myra was the only one who was enthusiastic about coming."

Greta quirked an eyebrow. "That's another one I can't quite figure out. I'd think the Carver farm would be the last place she'd want to work. Her husband is another casualty of Judson's hard heart. After they lost their farm to the bank, he shot himself. That was about twenty years ago."

"Maybe Miss Evangeline was just trying to undo some of her father's wicked decisions," I said. "Maybe she was kinder than she was given credit for."

Greta grinned. "You really liked her, didn't you?"

"I did," I agreed. "I liked her spunk. Myra seems happy at the farm, and she was certainly upset when Miss Evangeline turned up dead.

Jules doesn't seem to hold a grudge either. You didn't tell me he's Irish."

To my shock, Greta started giggling. The giggle turned to a laugh. Library patrons looked up from their books and stared. She laughed until tears ran down her face. At last, she grabbed a tissue, blew her nose, and gasped, "Oh, I should have warned you! So, he was Irish, was he?"

"Certainly," I said. "Surely you knew that."

She sank down on a chair and motioned for me to pull up another one.

Speaking just above a whisper, she said, "Jules is what you might call a bit different. He's a lot of fun, has a jolly disposition, and a vivid imagination. I guess ordinary, everyday life is too dull for him. He loves to read. Reads constantly. He likes to take on the leading character of whatever book appeals to him at the moment. He must have been reading a book based in Ireland. He's no more Irish than the man in the moon."

It took a few moments for that to sink in, then I smiled too.

"How original!" I said. "It would make life more fun, wouldn't it? I like Jules. Thanks for telling me about his little whims."

"I'll set three extra plates at the luncheon just in case we have the Carver people as guests," Greta said as I got up to leave.

"Grand!" I said in my best Irish brogue. "And I'll do m'best to prepare a scintillatin' little talk of some kind." I left the library grinning.

Chapter 23

I sat across from Ron Murray's desk as he shuffled some papers.

"Jackie isn't here today?" I asked to get the conversation going.

"No," he said. "We're having a guest for dinner tonight and she's out grocery shopping."

"Have you reached a decision on the document I gave you—the one Miss Evangeline and I signed?" I asked.

"If no one contests it, and in the absence of a will, it should hold up," he said. "No one from the Carver farm has been to see me, Ned. Maybe nobody was lurking around the corner after all, the night she talked to you about this." He picked up the paper in question and thumped it with his finger.

"If one of the Carvers had come to see you, that might just point the finger of guilt at them, mightn't it? If our conversation was overheard when Miss Evangeline and I signed that paper, somebody would know she was planning to consult you on it, and by coming to you, it would make him look guilty."

He nodded.

"You probably don't know that my dad and I were in the firm together when I graduated from law school. Then, Jackie and I moved to Oklahoma City. I set up practice there and she taught school. We came back to Ednalee after Dad passed away."

I hadn't realized Ron had begun his law practice with his father. This had happened while I was in Atlanta.

"I've been putting a lot of his old records into the computer," Ron said. "However, there was a fire a number of years ago and some records were destroyed. Dad kept a ledger and he had jotted notes about transactions—some transactions I can't find anywhere. For instance, there was Judson Carver. One of Dad's entries mentioned he had drawn up an irrevocable trust for Judson, but I can't find a copy of it anywhere, so I'm guessing it must have been destroyed in the fire."

I leaned toward his desk. "Irrevocable? Does that mean it can't be revoked, ever? Would it override Miss Evangeline's wishes?"

Ron drew a deep breath and frowned. "Depends upon the wording. And if it can't be found, it wouldn't matter anyway. I've checked the bank—you'd think the bank president would have a safety deposit box, but I guess he didn't. He was a suspicious old man, didn't trust anybody. My guess is if that document still exists, it's hidden somewhere in his house."

This was stunning news. I thought about the grand old mansion. How many rooms did it have? Was there a basement? An attic? Had the Carver relatives found the trust and destroyed it? Would that have been to their advantage? I had to find out.

"Look, Ned," Ron said, "I know you want to help. I know you have an oversized bump of curiosity, but leave this alone! Don't you realize that murders are committed with far less at stake than a multi-million-dollar estate? Let's just let this rock on. What is that ancient quote? *The wheels of justice turn slowly, but grind exceedingly fine.* Let the law handle everything surrounding Miss Evangeline and her will or her lack of one. You didn't know her. You shouldn't be concerned at all."

Feeling like a chastened younger sister, I stood up. Why did I want to get to the bottom of Miss Evangeline's death? Why did I want to make sure that her estate didn't fall into the hands of her murderer? Because the more I learned, the more I knew that some evil person had snatched life from an old, helpless woman, and maybe that same person had murdered her housekeeper as well. To my way of thinking, her cousins who lived on the estate were the chief suspects. I was determined that a murderer would not profit from his evil deed.

Chapter 24

"So your dinner guest was Mike, the boy Ron is trying to reroute before he gets into trouble with the law?" Pat asked Jackie as we sat in my dining room, coffee cups in hand. Rain sluiced down the windows, and the day was so chilly I had a small fire going in the fireplace.

"Yes," Jackie said. "And you know, he's not a bad kid. He was nervous, of course, anxious not to spill or break anything, but he was quiet and plainly looks up to Ron."

I held my coffee cup out of the way as Penny jumped onto my lap. "A caring adult can make a world of difference in a child's life," I said.

"Do you ever wonder about the background of criminals?" I asked nobody in particular. "I do. I mean the hardened, serial type. Where did they go wrong? Did they have nobody to love them, or does it take more than love to keep a young person from getting off to a bad start?"

"I think Cade's daughter Marianne is a prime example of the importance of a caring father. Marianne was still a child when Lena left her and Cade. But, under Cade's supervision, Marianne grew to be a wonderful young lady," Pat said.

"Cade and I have talked some about her and about Lena too," I told them. "I know he misses Marianne. I've never met her."

"You'll love her," Jackie assured me. "She's been on the mission field for so long, she has probably changed since I last saw her, but I'm sure she's still a sweet girl."

I was curious about Cade's marriage, but I would never question him. He would tell me what he wanted to tell me, and I determined not to push him.

We sipped our coffee, listening to rain pounding and an occasional clap of thunder. A stick in the fireplace burned in two, sending a shower of sparks up the chimney.

"I don't think any one particular reason causes a person to get in trouble," Pat said. "It may be a bunch of things or wrong decisions or a faulty view of life. I think everyone has a choice and, basically, knows when he chooses to do wrong. Each person is responsible for his own actions, and blaming society or circumstances is just an excuse."

A particularly hard clap of thunder caused us to jump.

"Did you ever see such a stormy month?" Pat asked. "I wonder if it has to do with the two full moons this month."

"*March, is this the reason that you're such a restless thing—you're not at home with winter and you're not at home with spring,*" I quoted from a poem I had learned in childhood.

"Isn't tomorrow the funeral for Miss Carver's housekeeper, Lila?" Jackie asked.

"It is," I said. "However, I don't plan to go. I didn't know the woman. I have other plans. You know, Judson Carver's irrevocable trust has disappeared. Ron thinks it may be somewhere in the mansion."

"Ned!" Pat said. "What are you planning? Please don't tell me you are going to break into that house."

Sometimes my friends amazed me. "Of course not," I said. "There may be someone there. I'd like to take food, maybe a casserole or a salad. Usually, someone stays behind to greet visitors or answer the phone. If I took a dish of something, I might be able to talk to someone and learn a bit more."

"About what?" Jackie asked. "Are you planning to ask if someone is ready to confess to Miss Evangeline's murder?"

Shaking my head, I said, "I don't think anyone who would kill a helpless old woman would be bothered too much by a conscience. I thought perhaps in the absence of the family, there might be a gossipy neighbor who wouldn't mind talking to me. I don't know that family—just impressions of them are all I have. But, I'd really like to find out if anybody is even aware that Judson Carver made a trust once, long ago, and that nobody knows what he did with it."

Jackie narrowed her eyes. "Are you considering maybe doing a personal search? I think that would be like looking for a needle in a haystack. You don't know if a trust is still in existence and, if it is, you have no idea where it might be. The Carver house is mighty big and mighty old and probably has a lot of possible hiding places."

My friends' lack of enthusiasm was dampening my spirits. "Of course, you're right," I said meekly.

"Surely you wouldn't go inside that empty old house if no one is there," Pat said, her eyes as big as saucers. "It may be fabulous, but it gives me the creeps. You wouldn't think of prying up a window to get in or something crazy, would you?"

"Well, rats! Of course not. I have a healthy respect for the law."

"The luncheon is in just a couple more days," Jackie said. "You'll have ample opportunity to talk to the Carver women then."

Subdued, I nodded. "Yes."

"It looks like the rain isn't letting up," Pat said. "I plan to stop at Coradee's on the way home, so I'd better be going. Remember, Ned, don't do anything foolish. Okay?"

"Okay," I agreed, feeling hurt that they would suspect me of such a thing.

I walked with them to the door. "Where is your sense of adventure?" I asked. "One for all and all for one? The girls I remember were always ready for an exciting excursion."

Pat grinned and gave me a hug. "When we were young and foolish, we weren't afraid to jump in where angels fear to tread."

"But, we're older now and wiser," Jackie added. "Just stay away from the Carver mansion, Ned."

I waved as they drove off through the rain. True, my idea was a foolish one. Why should I think I could find a document that had been hidden by a devious old man years ago? However, if given the chance, Lila's funeral would sure be a good time to look.

Chapter 25

The rain had stopped by the next morning. I whipped up a pan of homemade lasagna to take with me to the Carver farm. Yes, I had decided to try my luck at finding someone there to talk to. Perhaps a member of the family or a chatty neighbor would have stayed behind to take phone calls from friends or to accept a condolence dish of food. And, just maybe that same someone would offer a bit of information about the people on the estate—their backgrounds, or how they got along with Miss Evangeline.

Funny how I hadn't traveled the road to the Carver place in more than forty years and now, it was becoming quite familiar to me. Leaving my Escape in the parking area, I walked between wet shrubs until I was, once again, at the impressive gray door. I rapped with the brass knocker and waited. No one came to answer my knock. Cautiously, I tried the door. It was unlocked.

Pushing the door open, I stepped inside. The hall was dark and shadowy. "Hello?" I called softly. The house seemed listening and empty. Why had I never noticed the painting of the middle-aged man whose clothes were plainly from a previous century which hung on the wall? Had it been hanging there the other times I was here? And why did his eyes seem to look directly into mine?

Giving myself a mental shake, I tore my gaze from that unnerving portrait. This trip was evidently wasted, but nothing ventured, nothing gained. I'd take my lasagna and go home. Miss Evangeline believed in ghosts. I didn't, but if they were real, I could think of no better place to haunt than this ancient mansion.

As I turned to leave, a faint sound came from somewhere within the house. Was that a footstep? Perhaps someone was home after all. Maybe somebody was in the kitchen and hadn't heard my knock.

"Hello?" I called again, my voice echoing in the vastness.

I tiptoed down the hall. For some reason, the atmosphere of the house seemed to call for stealth. I would check the kitchen and, if no one was there, I'd leave.

The kitchen was empty of human life and it seemed cold to me. No fragrant aroma of coffee greeted me, no welcome light shone from overhead. The gray light of day seeped through the windows. A kitchen should be the heart of a house. It should have felt warm and inviting, as it had the first time I was here and met Miss Evangeline. But today, it was a lonely, dreary place.

Admitting defeat, I decided to leave my offering of food, scribble a note that I had been here, and go. But, on second thought, should I do that? Would the family wonder why I had felt free to come inside the house when they were not at home? Perhaps I'd better not write the note and no one would know I had come. I'd take the lasagna with me and count this a useless trip. My idea about searching this house for the lost trust seemed silly and far-fetched, now that I was here. I would have no idea where to begin. Besides, I really wasn't into home intrusion and, as Pat said, the house was a bit on the creepy side.

I had no trouble identifying the sound that I heard next. It was definitely a footstep. There was no denying that I was not alone in the house and someone was coming my way. Wildly, I looked around for another way out. Wasn't there a kitchen door? In my panic, I couldn't see one. With no escape visible, I would have to hide. Explaining my presence in this house would be a little sticky and I didn't want to try to convince anyone I was here innocently.

The pantry seemed my only option, but it would work only as long as no one entered it. Did the pantry have an outside door? I pictured myself crouching beside a shelf of canned food, waiting for a chance to leave.

The fireplace! It was huge with an inglenook built into one side. An antique chair sat in this area. In olden days, it would have been a cozy place to keep warm and read or knit.

I tiptoed to the chair, squeezed around it, and hunkered down behind it. The footsteps came closer. If this unknown person happened to look my way, he would see me crouching there. And if he didn't, he'd surely hear my pounding heart. I had forgotten to take the lasagna with me into my hiding place and there was no time to retrieve it.

Pressing my hand against my mouth, I stifled a scream as a tall, dark man strode into the kitchen. Mick Morrow—the arrogant man who had interrupted Jules and me in the garden. I got a good look at his chiseled face and hooked nose. He might be Pearly's brother, but they did not resemble in the least.

He glanced at the dish of lasagna, shrugged, and began pulling open drawers in the kitchen. I breathed a sigh of relief. Maybe he thought Myra had left the dish there.

The dark kitchen was in my favor, and I prayed he would not turn on a light. He opened the doors under the sink, gave a quick glance, and moved to the fireplace. Kneeling down on the hearth, he ran his fingers over the bricks. He was looking for something. As he moved closer to the inglenook, I prayed silently, asking the Lord to hide me.

Standing up, he turned his head toward the window. I heard it too. A car was approaching. Had Lila's funeral ended? As softly as a cat, Mick left the kitchen and disappeared somewhere within the house.

I took a deep breath. I was in a tight place with little room to move. Pushing against the inglenook's brick wall to give myself leverage, I stood up. The brick under my hand moved. What? Was the mortar so aged it was crumbling? I heard a door open. I would have no chance to check out the masonry in this old fireplace. Voices came down the hall, only two voices: Pearly's and a man's, possibly Elbert's. Knowing I was trapped, I tried to gather my rattled wits and think of an excuse for being here. Or, should I return to my hiding place? But, the voices moved away from me and up the stairs. Could I manage to go back down the hall and out the front door undetected?

I picked up my dish of lasagna and tiptoed from the kitchen. Sidling along the wall, I reached the front door and eased it open. So far, so good. Closing the door behind me, I trotted down the steps and along the path to my car, thanking the Lord that the family had used the back driveway and also for the cloudy day and my black SUV, hard to spot in the gloom. Climbing inside, I turned the key and slowly drove down the driveway toward the road. I shook all the way back to my house and didn't stop shaking until I was safely inside my own kitchen, a cup of chamomile tea in my hands with Penny on my lap and Ulysses keeping watch. Decidedly, I wasn't cut out to be an undercover agent. It would have been too hard on my heart. But, how would I get back into the house to check out the loose brick in the fireplace? Or, was it just one of many bricks that had loosened with the centuries?

Chapter 26

I was pleased to see so many people at Greta's Old Houses luncheon. Miss Ann was there with notes in hand, ready to give her talk about Ednalee's early settlers and their homes. Daisy Stanton, Coradee, Pat, Jackie, and all three of the women from the Carver farm were present. Myra, Veda, and Pearly looked a bit ill at ease but seemed friendly enough and happy to have been invited.

We were seated informally around Greta's table. Most of the guests had finished eating when Greta asked Miss Ann to talk. I loved hearing about Ednalee's early settlers and the first homes built in our area, many of them still occupied.

Everyone had eaten their dessert by the time Miss Ann sat down. The Carver group had listened attentively. Veda even made a few comments.

"Greta, I certainly like your house. Quite old and probably historic, isn't it?"

Greta smiled. "Thank you. Yes, it is. My house and its history are what piqued my interest in starting the Old Houses Club."

Veda nodded. "I like historic houses. Has your house been involved in anything dark and nefarious in the past?"

Greta raised her eyebrows. "Hmm. I'm not sure about that. Nothing that I know of."

I stood and smiled at the group. I'd hint at a few things without giving anything away. This was my chance to let the women from the

Carver farm know that I was no threat, but I felt it was also an opportunity to needle a conscience that might be feeling a bit of remorse.

"As you know, Ednalee is an old town, and old towns have some historic mysteries," I said. "Our town is no exception. Some of its history I learned from my family, some I gathered by reading, and some I learned by talking to people. You see, as well as a history, Ednalee has a few secrets."

This got everyone's attention. I spoke about the legend of buried gold, about bank robbers who were said to have hidden out in our area during the turbulent 1930s, and about a few unsolved murders.

"I've heard it said that walls have ears." I'd try to be subtle and maybe stir a little curiosity. Although I dared not say so, I wondered if, in particular, the Carver mansion had a pair of listening ears the night Miss Evangeline floored me with her assertion that someone was trying to kill her. "If they do, the walls of all the old houses in our area must really be burning. If only they could talk as well as listen.

"But," I continued, "sometimes folk with a guilty conscience have to confide in someone, and maybe it's my honest face"—I paused here while a ripple of laughter ran through my audience—"but for some reason, people share their secrets with me. I've been told several things, but I'm pretty good about not repeating gossip. I'm sure a lot of what I've heard is just that—gossip or somebody's guesswork. I pay no attention to it and promptly forget it."

There! That should have been clear enough to anyone who thought I was a threat that I didn't believe Miss Evangeline's story about someone trying to kill her.

As I sat down, I glanced at Myra, Veda, and Pearly. They looked thoughtful, and Myra's face was flushed. Did one of them harbor a guilty conscience or some dangerous information?

"I was wondering, Ned, whether your home holds any secrets. I assume it's as old as this one?" asked Pearly.

"It is," I answered. "The house has been in my family for generations and was willed to me by my Uncle Javin. The townsfolk call it Granger Mansion, but in no way does it compare to the Carver mansion. My house is much smaller. Yes, I believe it has held a secret or two but, as far as I know, they have all been put to rest."

Pearly smiled and pushed back her perfectly-coiffed hair. "That's interesting. Some people are so intrigued by houses that have been lived in for generations, that they enjoy searching through them to see what might lie buried beneath floorboards or hidden back in a cabinet."

This conversation was beginning to get uncomfortable. Pearly wore a calculating expression as she stared at me. Did she know I had been in her house the day of Lila's funeral? Had she glanced out of a window and seen me?

I helped Greta clear the table. After stacking plates in the sink, I turned around and nearly bumped into Myra. She was blinking rapidly and her face, which had appeared flushed earlier, was now a decided beet red.

"Ned, I liked what you said about keeping secrets. I know a few too, and I think it'd be safer if somebody else besides me knew them. You see, I'm sort of like the man who had a bear by the tail. I don't want to stay on at the Carver place with Miss Evangeline gone, but I'm afraid to leave."

"Goodness, Myra, what are you afraid of? Can you tell me?" I asked, putting my hand on her arm.

"Yes. No. I mean I can tell you, but not here and not now. Do you think you could come to my house and talk to me, maybe tomorrow night? I'll be at the mansion until after supper, but come any time after seven. And please don't let any of the Carvers know you're coming."

"Sure," I said, trying not to show my excitement that my talk was having some results. "Just tell me where you live."

She gave me directions then turned to go back to the dining room.

I stopped her. "Miss Evangeline—she said some pretty surprising things the time I came to her house, the night before she died. Do you think she might have been getting a bit senile?"

Myra opened her mouth to answer, but at that moment, Pearly walked into the kitchen with a load of coffee cups.

"I can answer that," Pearly said. "Yes, she was senile, sad to say. She imagined things. Believed in ghosts and all that. I hope she didn't tell you any wild tales."

According to the coroner's report about Miss Evangeline's death, I'd say the story she told me about somebody wanting her dead had been quite truthful. Evidently, the sheriff hadn't chosen to share this information with the Carvers. I smiled. "Well, yes, she did tell me a few, but I didn't believe them. I'm sure she had an active imagination, but then, most people do."

Surely this would be enough to let them know I was no threat. And, actually, I was being truthful. The part I didn't believe was the story about ghosts living at the mansion.

"But not to the extent poor Evangeline had," Pearly said. "Myra, are you ready to thank our hostess and leave? We have a lot to do back at the house." She turned toward me. "You know how it is after a death—papers to go through, things to put away."

"I understand that," I said. "Do you and Elbert and Veda plan to stay on at the house?"

Pearly smiled. "Oh, yes. That's just what Evangeline told us she wanted us to do, in the event we outlived her. We are her next of kin, you know."

What did she mean? Were they going to file a claim in court? Is that how things were done when someone died without a will? At least, now I knew their intentions were to stick like leeches to the Carver farm. What did people say about possession being nine-tenths of the law? Hopefully, that would not be the case with Miss Evangeline's farm.

Chapter 27

"How am I going to be able to check out the loose brick in the fireplace at the Carver home?" I asked Ulysses. "Was it loose because of age, or could it be a hiding place?"

Ulysses laid his head on my knee and stared at me with soulful brown eyes.

"I know," I said. "You're perfectly willing to help."

I could think of no possible excuse for going back to the Carver house. I couldn't just show up and say I had come for tea. Would Myra know anything about the loose brick? After all, the kitchen was her domain. Tonight, I'd try to sound her out without telling her I had found it.

Would she know what Pearly and Elbert were planning? Or Veda? Was Myra ready to confess to murdering Miss Evangeline, or did she know who had?

What had Cade learned? I hadn't heard from him since he called telling me Ken was gone. And what about Ken? Why did he leave without letting anyone know? He certainly looked guilty, but I couldn't believe he was so heartless as to murder Miss Evangeline. Then, there was the death of Lila Fletcher. Were we dealing with two murderers? It seemed far more likely that her rant at Miss Evangeline's funeral was the direct reason she'd had to die. Surely, it was only one murderer who wanted to make sure Lila didn't tell anybody of her suspicions.

Perhaps I should try to talk to Jules again. He seemed the most approachable of anyone at the mansion. I smiled, thinking of his alias. When I saw him again, who would he be? Did he ever revert to being Jules Thatcher or was it more fun to take on the persona of someone from his favorite book?

The hours seemed to go slowly, but I felt elated. Maybe at last I was making headway on ferreting out the murderer. Even another rainstorm couldn't dampen my spirits. At last I was going to talk to someone who was close to Miss Evangeline—someone who seemed to want to tell me something important. I decided to start a little early for Myra's house. If she hadn't finished her chores at the mansion, I would sit in the car and wait.

The ringing phone stopped me as I picked up my purse and started for the door.

Caller ID showed *Unknown Caller*. Usually, I ignored this type of call, but something prompted me to pick up the receiver.

"Mrs. McNeil?" a guttural voice asked.

I had learned not to answer with a 'yes' because if the caller happened to be a telemarketer, I might inadvertently be agreeing to who knows what.

"Who is this?" I asked.

"Never mind," said the voice. "Just stay out of what doesn't concern you. Keep away from Myra Edwards. She's dangerous. She's the one who killed Miss Evangeline. She's planning to kill you too. Be smart and just stay home tonight."

A click came through the line and then the dial tone.

My scalp prickled. Slowly, I replaced the receiver. Who in the world was that? Somebody was warning me away from my appointment with Myra, but why? Was what the caller said true? Was Myra the murderer? And who knew about the appointment? Had someone overheard us at the luncheon or had Myra told somebody I was coming?

I hesitated between the phone and my purse, staring into space, trying to assimilate the call. Evidently the caller had disguised his voice. It must have been a man. Surely a woman's voice would not be as coarse.

One thing was obvious—someone didn't want me talking to Myra. I doubted that the caller was really concerned about my safety. The phone message was a threat. Remembering Myra's hurried words and the fear evident in her face, I felt she had been telling me the truth. She was afraid of someone at Carver mansion. She knew something that was a danger to her. Even now, waiting for me to show up at her house, she was probably as nervous as I.

The caller had told me to be smart and stay home, so I would do the opposite. I had to know why I had been warned. Picking up my purse, I walked to the door and got into my car. Maybe Myra held the key to this puzzle. I was determined to find out.

Chapter 28

The rain stopped and I turned off my windshield wipers. About halfway to Myra's home, I realized no one in the whole world knew where I was and that was not a good thing. I speed-dialed Cade but got no answer, only his voice mail. Leaving a message, I told him where I'd be. Hopefully, he wouldn't be away from his phone long. I wouldn't tell Jackie or Pat my plans. They would only worry.

A nearly full moon peered fitfully from between scudding clouds. A blustery wind buffeted my car, swaying the tree branches that reached toward the road. It was a wild sort of night, typical for March.

Turning onto the Carvers' long driveway, I slowed, searching the woods until I saw the narrow lane that led to Myra's house. She had said her house was within walking distance from the mansion and she usually took a footpath, but I, coming from town, should surely come upon it soon.

My car's headlights picked out a small, white frame building nestled in a grove of trees. Stopping in front of it, I turned off the car's engine and looked for a welcoming light. The windows reflected only my car's headlights. Was Myra not back from the Carver place yet? I would wait a few minutes before knocking. The sun had set about thirty minutes ago and darkness was closing in. Surely, it took only a few minutes for Myra to walk home after she had finished preparing supper at the Carver house and cleaning up the kitchen afterward.

My eagerness overcame my intention to wait. Grabbing my flashlight from the dash, I opened the car door and closed it as quietly as possible. Walking up to the front door, I knocked. And knocked again. Nobody came to welcome me. I tried the doorknob. Locked. Flicking on my light, I shone it around the yard.

Could Myra be outside somewhere? Could she have fallen? Or, was her invitation to me only a ruse? Maybe she had had no intention of talking to me and was back at the mansion, laughing at my gullibility.

I cautiously walked around the house. The yard was neat with well-kept flower beds. Tree frogs trilled from the woods and somewhere, an owl hooted. Completing my circuit of the house, I stood once more on the front porch, undecided about what to do next. Should I forget about talking to Myra and go back home?

Directing the flashlight's beam through the windows only resulted in its reflection. I couldn't see inside the house. Perhaps Myra had been held up at the big house for some reason and was late in keeping her appointment. I was a little early, so I'd try to curb my impatience.

Sitting down on the porch, I waited until it became pretty obvious that Myra wasn't coming. The best thing to do would be to go to the mansion and see if she was still there. Getting back into my SUV and driving would be quicker, but that would alert whoever was in the house of my presence. Myra had specified coming to her house and not telling anyone of my visit. So, I would walk to the mansion as Myra did each day to and from work.

It wasn't hard to find the path to the big house. It began at the edge of the yard where the woods ended. The trees were not fully leafed yet and through their branches, I could see the lights of the much larger Carver home, surely no more than a quarter of a mile away. There was the awful possibility that Myra might have fallen on that path or that somebody had injured her. My pace quickened.

My flashlight's beam had no trouble picking out the well-worn trail. Trees pressed in on either side and the wind moaning through them sounded like voices from another world. Sternly, I reminded myself that no wolves or mountain lions lived in these parts anymore. At least,

I had not heard of a sighting. These animals preferred a solitary life, far away from civilization. I hoped.

The path ended at the edge of the mansion's yard. Hedges and flower gardens cast flitting shadows as I crept past them. The dark silhouettes of barns loomed in the distance and the well-lit house sat just in front of me. Should I go to the back door and knock? Myra had asked me not to tell anyone of our planned meeting. I couldn't imagine that the Carvers would be happy about it.

Taking a deep breath, I shrugged and prepared to go back the way I had come. Myra wasn't at her house and she wasn't anywhere between there and the big house. After my excitement at possibly learning something from her, I felt deflated. This was evidently a wild goose chase. I'd try to talk to her another time.

As I turned around, I heard a noise somewhere nearby, just past the herb garden.

"Myra?" I called in a semi-whisper. "Are you there?"

There was no mistaking it this time. "I'm here. Help me. Please."

My heart in my mouth, I started in the direction of the voice. My flashlight's beam picked out the herb garden and gazebo. Again, I heard it. Not words this time, just a faint moan as if someone were in pain. And then, "The maze."

An involuntary shudder born of an old fear ran through me. The maze? If Myra was in the maze, I had little chance of finding her. I hated that place. It stretched before me in the gloom like a menacing snake, the entrance an open mouth, taunting me.

"Wait," I called. "I'll go for help. Are you hurt?"

Another moan and the voice was fainter. "No time. Hurry."

I took one step into the maze, then another. My heart pounded so loudly I nearly missed the voice when it spoke again.

"Hurry."

Taking a few more steps between boxwood walls, I shone my light wildly around me. "I'm here," I said. "I don't know if I can find you."

No sound at all met my statement, nothing except the rustle of the wind through ancient shrubs as I crept deeper into the web of boxwood.

111

If only I had brought Ulysses with me. Surely, he could have scented out Myra within these serpentine walls. If only I had asked Pat or Jackie to come. But, I had done neither, and now here I was in a place I had feared since childhood, trying to locate a bodiless voice somewhere in the darkness.

Chapter 29

Where was the person calling to me? Now that I was inside the maze, if the unseen person would keep talking, maybe I'd be able to find her.

Throwing caution to the wind, I called, "Myra! Where are you?"

The voice seemed directionless, just a moan somewhere ahead, or was it to the side? By this time, I was deep into the maze. What was it Jackie had said so many years ago? Something about always taking the right-hand turn when the paths diverged. The only trouble was, I didn't know how many exits I had already passed. My only thought had been to find that wispy voice.

But now, I heard a new sound, and it was decidedly behind me. Footsteps! Someone was following me. Fear raced up and down my spine. I held my breath to listen. Someone was coming after me— someone I could hear but not see. Was it the same person who had called for help? Had this been a trick to get me into the maze?

Panic took over. Whoever was following me surely was up to no good. I ran blindly, the reaching limbs of boxwood scratching my arms, not knowing where I was, knowing only that I didn't want my pursuer to catch me.

"Wait! Stop!" a man's voice called.

Fat chance. That was the last thing I would do. I banged into a dead end, whirled, and started down another tunnel. In my headlong flight, I didn't see the object on the ground until I stumbled over it. Gasping,

I shone my light downward where lay the prostrate body of Myra Edwards.

Shock and disbelief squeezed my heart. What had happened? Hadn't she been calling me? Her face, in the glow from my flashlight, looked white. A dark pool of blood spread around her head, and there was an awful stillness about her.

Dropping to my knees, I felt for a pulse. There was none. Her skin felt cold to my touch.

"Miss Ned! Why were you running? What are you doing here?"

I gasped and whirled around as Jules Thatcher burst into view. He stopped when he saw me. He was dressed in dirty gardening clothes. His eyes were wide, and I had the feeling that this time Jules Thatcher was not impersonating anyone.

My chest hurt. My throat hurt and I could barely croak out the question. "Jules! Why were you chasing me? Myra or somebody was calling me. She needed help. Did you hear her?"

Jules shook his head. "No, no, I didn't." He put his hand on Myra's wrist. "It wasn't Myra either. She has been dead for quite some time. Was somebody in the maze calling you?"

Tears slid down my cheeks and my chin shook so badly I could hardly speak.

"Yes. Somebody. I heard somebody asking for help. I was supposed to meet Myra at her house. Somebody killed her, Jules. Did you know she was dead?"

He shook his head and swiped a hand across his perspiring forehead. "No," he said. "I didn't know. But, I saw you go into the maze. It's a dangerous place. Easy to get lost. Come on, Miss Ned. You're in shock and neither of us can help Myra. We need to get the sheriff."

He pulled me to my feet. "But, I don't know the way out," I sobbed. My legs felt like water.

Putting his arm around my shoulders, he led me away from that still form on the ground. "It's all right," he said. "I know the way. You're safe now."

Chapter 30

As I thought back on that awful night, I couldn't remember much about what happened between the time Jules and I left the maze and went through the back door into the Carver mansion until Cade drove me home. I knew that Jules phoned the sheriff, and I guess Sheriff Cordray must have phoned Cade. Or, maybe Cade heard the call from the dispatcher or picked up my phone message. As much as I had longed to see the rooms of that fabulous mansion, later I recalled very little of the lovely area where Elbert, Pearly, Jules, Veda, Mick Morrow, and I waited while, one by one, the sheriff took us aside and questioned us. I had a dim impression of floor-to-ceiling bookcases, a large fireplace, and a bright chandelier hanging from a high ceiling.

I did remember that Cade drove my SUV home while Gerald followed with Cade's truck. Both men walked me into my living room. Gerald heated milk for hot chocolate while Cade sat beside me on the sofa.

"You went to see Myra because she had invited you?" Cade questioned. The sheriff had asked me the same thing.

Wearily, I nodded. "She did. It was something about Miss Evangeline's death. She was frightened, Cade, but she didn't tell me of whom. It was awful. I went into the maze because I thought she was calling me. I heard someone. Somebody wanted me to go into the maze."

"Could it have been Jules?" Gerald asked, handing me the mug of cocoa.

I shook my head. "It was a woman. Why did she want me in the maze?"

"Whoever it was wanted you to find Myra," Cade said. "She knew you'd be shocked. Myra's death was a warning to you to keep out of the investigation into Miss Evangeline's murder. And, of course, to keep Myra from telling you whatever she had on her mind."

I shivered and pulled the afghan closer. "If Jules hadn't seen me go into the maze, if he hadn't followed me in, who knows what would have happened. He was as shocked as I was to find her. Cade, how did Myra die? There was so much blood around her head."

"Somebody clubbed her to death," Cade answered. "She died in the same way Miss Carver did. Myra either went into that maze trying to escape her murderer or she was lured in, as you were."

With the hot drink in my hands and the afghan around my shoulders, I finally got warm, but the image of Myra, lying white and still within that maze, would not go away.

"Poor Myra," I said, biting my lips to keep from crying. "She must have been terrified. She knew who the murderer was, Cade. She planned to tell me."

He nodded. "She either knew or strongly suspected."

Gerald ran his hand through his hair. "What a motley crew that was tonight—all of them declaring their innocence, but I wouldn't put murder past any of them, 'specially that shifty-eyed guy with the greasy-looking hair. What was his name?"

Cade grimaced. "Mick Morrow."

I put my empty mug on the floor. Penny came to investigate it. "Pearly said he's her brother, but he doesn't look anything like her."

One corner of Cade's mouth turned up. "He's not her brother. His picture was on a law enforcement memo that made its rounds last year, after that casino was raided up north. Morrow works for a gambling syndicate."

Could this awful night get any more shocking? "A gambling syndicate? What's he doing at the Carver farm? Surely, they wouldn't try to turn that lovely estate into a big casino, would they?"

Cade shook his head. "Maybe. Maybe not. I doubt that's the reason he's there."

How much more did Cade know that he hadn't been willing to share with me?

"Cade Morris, do you know why he's there?"

"I have my suspicions, but there's another angle or two I need to check first," Cade answered, rising to his feet.

I got up to walk Cade and Gerald to the door and lock it after them.

"I'm sure about one thing," I said. "Somebody in that room tonight was a murderer."

Cade shook his head. "I'm not sure of that, Ned. You're leaving out someone else who has a lot of explaining to do. He's pretty high on my list of suspects."

"Who's that?" I asked.

"Ken Riley," Cade answered. "The missing Ken Riley. I know you think he's innocent, but an innocent man doesn't run away."

Before I could think of a retort, he reminded me to keep my doors locked, then he and Gerald went down the steps, got into Cade's truck, and drove off into the night.

Chapter 31

The sun shone through my kitchen windows. The day was calm and serene, making the violence of last night seem like simply a bad dream. Pat, Jackie, and I sat at my table, enjoying coffee and a plate of shortbread I had baked using the recipe Miss Ann gave me. Pat shook her head and squinted her eyes as she stared at me, a sure sign that she was not happy.

"So, Ned, do you have a death wish or something?" she asked.

I studied my napkin and continued pleating it into a lovely ruffle. "Why would you ask a silly thing like that?"

"She means you insist on getting involved in first one scrape and then another," Jackie said. They were, of course, referring to the part I played in the drama at the Carver farm last night.

Frowning, I said, "I know what she means, but if I had told you about Myra's invitation, you would have tried to talk me out of going or insisted on coming with me."

"As it turns out, neither of those things would have been a bad idea," Pat said.

"We're just alarmed for you, Ned," Jackie said in a softer tone. "You could have been killed last night just as poor Myra was. You really need to use more caution. Promise you will in the future?"

Drawing a deep breath, I said, "Okay, I promise. I just didn't want to involve anybody else. If you had gone with me, it wouldn't have changed the outcome and you would have been in danger."

"Just as you were?" Pat asked.

"I *felt* that I was," I admitted. "But, I really don't *know* that I was. Myra's murderer might have just wanted me to find her body. He was probably out of the maze by the time Jules found me."

"Gerald said that Moe Decker is loose, but I don't think he has ever been murderous," Pat said. "He's mean as the Devil would want him, but what reason would he have for murdering those three women?"

I shook my head.

Pat gazed into space. "This makes three murders. Bad things happen in threes. I hope that nobody else who is concerned with this will die. This month and its two full moons is almost over. I'll be so glad to see April get here."

"Let's hope," I said. "Pretty soon we are going to run out of suspects."

Jackie took another sip of coffee. "Jules Thatcher was certainly Johnny-on-the-spot last night. Do you think he could have killed Miss Evangeline as well as Lila Fletcher and Myra? Maybe he was only pretending he didn't know about Myra, just to appear innocent."

Pat looked horrified. "Not Jules Thatcher, Jackie. How could you think that? He's Greta's cousin and there's not a nicer person in the world than Greta."

"He isn't Greta's cousin," Jackie said. "He's her husband's cousin. Besides, he may have had a motive. Judson Carver took his family's home, way back when, and his father died shortly after. Jules and his mother had a hard time making a living, all thanks to Judson Carver."

"If you are saying that could be a reason to murder Miss Evangeline, I don't think so," I said. "If he had such a murderous resentment, why didn't he kill her a long time ago? Why stay on at the farm? He even told me that there were times he and Miss Evangeline shared a night-time glass of wine. That doesn't sound to me like he hated her."

"Maybe he was just biding his time," Jackie said. "Maybe he's been laying his plans all these years. You know how an old grudge is—it festers and grows and sometimes doesn't ever go away."

"I agree with Pat," I said. "He may have saved my life last night. He followed me into the maze and guided me out. I'm grateful to him."

I put my piece of shortbread on my napkin. It wouldn't go down past the lump in my throat.

"Ron said that Judson Carver made some sort of trust. But, there was a fire during Ron's dad's time and now he doesn't have a copy of it," I said. "Judson's copy may have been destroyed or it may be in his house somewhere. If only I'd had time to look behind that loose brick in the fireplace."

"What?" Pat yelled. "What about a loose brick in the fireplace?"

Too late, I realized I hadn't shared that particular escapade with my friends. Neither had I told Cade. I was afraid none of them would understand, but confession was good for the soul. I don't know how good it was for friendships, but I confessed I had taken lasagna to the Carvers and had nearly been caught by Mick Morrow.

Jackie shook her head as I finished my tale. "The only thing to do, Ned, is to tell Cade and see if he can get a search warrant for the place. The trust could be hiding anywhere in the house. It may not be important at all. It's old—would have to be."

Pat shook her head. "Cade can't call for a search warrant unless he has a good reason. Now, I'll admit that loose brick sounds suspicious, but Ned, you'll have to tell Cade how you know it's there."

"I realize that," I said. "He's already told me to leave these murders to law enforcement, so I think I'll just live with a guilty conscience and not confess any more misdeeds."

Pat looked at me and shook her head. "You know, you might feel a lot better if you'd quit chalking up so many misdeeds. Then you wouldn't have anything to confess."

True, I had quite a bit to tell Cade if, someday, I deemed it the best thing to do, but I really had no control over the unexpected arrival of just one more problem that happened after Pat and Jackie had gone home, and in broad daylight too.

Chapter 32

I've always thought better with a pencil in my hand. I had just written the label "Suspects" on a sheet of paper when my brass door knocker echoed through the house. Ulysses rose to his feet, a low growl in his throat.

"It's all right, Ulysses," I told him. "Come along with me and we'll see who's here."

Peeking out of the window, I saw Ken Riley standing on my front porch. He was dressed in jeans, a denim jacket, scuffed boots, and a western hat. His shoulders slumped. He looked tired.

"Ken!" I cried, pulling open the door and staring at him. "Where on earth have you been? Did you know Cade and the sheriff and everybody are looking for you? Why did you run away? Why are you here? What's going on?"

He grinned sheepishly. "Hi there, Ned. I didn't run away, but . . . May I come in and explain?"

For a moment, I stood staring at him while a dozen thoughts raced through my mind. Why hadn't he gone straight to Cade? Why come to me? And why had he popped up the day after Myra's murder? Should I let him in?

Ulysses sniffed Ken's jeans, his tail tentatively wagging. All right. Ulysses was not afraid, and neither was I. Ken had always seemed honest to me, a trustworthy person.

"Sure," I said. "Come in. But, this had better be good."

He stepped inside, removed his hat, looked around at the entry with its old-fashioned furnishings, and gave a low whistle.

"So, this is what Javin's house looks like," he said softly. "Quite a place."

"It is," I agreed. "Come to the kitchen and I'll get you a cup of coffee."

I motioned for him to sit down at the table and poured a cup of coffee for him and another for myself. Ulysses lay down on the floor under the table. Ken quickly drained his cup.

"Thanks," he said. "I've been driving a while. It's a long trip from Kentucky."

Ken had a lot of things to clear up, and directness, as my mama used to say, is a virtue. "Did you know Myra died yesterday?" I asked.

He blinked, shock widening his eyes. "Myra? No. Why? How? Don't tell me she was murdered!"

I nodded. "Yes. In the same way as was Miss Evangeline."

He sat for a moment, digesting this news. Drawing a long breath, he said, "At least I can't be blamed for that. I was on the road last night. I stopped to fill the truck with gas somewhere. I'm sure I kept the receipt."

"Good. If you just had told the sheriff or Cade everything about Miss Evangeline's death at first, you wouldn't be a suspect now. But, you didn't tell them she was alive when you found her or that you turned her over. You didn't try to get help. And then, you took off. That made you look guilty."

"I don't know why I didn't tell them right away," he said. "I guess, since I found her, I was afraid it'd look bad for me, but I just made things worse."

"You did," I agreed. "Why did you run away, Ken? You said you went to Kentucky? Why? And why did you come back?"

He stared at his cup, turning it around and around. Without looking up, he said, "I went home. I told you my dad is dead and Mom is in a nursing facility with Alzheimer's. Sometimes Mom doesn't know who I am nor who she is, for that matter, and sometimes her mind is as clear as a bell. I needed to talk to her. I've had my suspicions for a long time, and I wanted some honest answers."

Okay. So he went home to Kentucky. I could understand the need to go home, to connect with loved ones. I had felt the same way when I made the trek from Georgia to Oklahoma when Uncle Javin asked me to come. He was my last living relative, but he died a few minutes after I got here. However, Ken could have chosen a more judicious time to make that trip.

He took a long, white envelope from his jacket's pocket and handed it to me. "Read this," he said. "It'll explain a lot."

"What is it?" I asked, pulling a legal-looking document out of the envelope.

"Just read it," Ken said.

It was a birth certificate. I read it. And read it again. This was too much to take in. I gave it back to Ken and stared at him for a moment, stunned to the core. I would never have guessed Miss Evangeline's secret. "You were adopted?" I whispered. "Your birth parents were Miss Evangeline Carver and Javin Granger?"

He nodded, refolded the certificate, and slid it back into its envelope.

"You do believe this birth certificate is the real thing, don't you?" he asked.

I swallowed a gulp of coffee, choked, and coughed into my napkin. "I suppose I'll have to, won't I? Right now I'm in a state of shock, Ken. Please explain."

"During one of her lucid moments, Mom told me the story. She and Miss Evangeline had been friends when they were young. When Miss Evangeline wound up 'in trouble' as Mom put it, her father, Judson, was scandalized. He made her go away to have her baby—me— and give me up for adoption. Mom and Dad were childless, and they agreed to take me. Miss Evangeline kept up with me through the years, sending money for college and a lot of extras. Then, when Mom went into the home, Miss Evangeline asked me to come and work on the farm." He gazed through my kitchen window. "I always wondered why I got such a generous salary for my work. I guess now I know."

Why hadn't I seen it before, his resemblance to my uncle? His head shape, his eyes, all were pure Javin Granger.

"But, why didn't my uncle claim you?" I asked. "It just doesn't sound like him to shirk his responsibility. I'd have thought he would be so proud of you, and surely he would have married Miss Evangeline."

Ken shook his head. "Mom said he didn't know. And Judson, my— my grandfather, didn't want the family name connected to somebody who was accused of murder. It seems Javin went to the penitentiary before I was born."

Tears flooded my eyes. "That means we're cousins! I thought I didn't have any family left and suddenly, here you are." I slid from my chair and came around the table to stand by him. He stood up, put his arms around me, and I gave my newfound family a tight hug.

"Hi, Cousin," he said. "I'm sorry that I seem to be following in Javin's footsteps, accused of murder just as he was."

Wiping my eyes, I said, "But, you are innocent, and I am going to prove you are. Ken, do you realize that this house should rightfully be yours?"

"What? Do you mean Granger Mansion?" he asked, gazing around the kitchen.

"I do. You're Javin's son."

He laughed. "And you are goofy if you think I want your home. I'm sure you have a deed, and somebody told me Javin willed the whole thing to you. I sure don't want to go into a court battle to take away your home. It's yours. I don't want it."

With shaking hands, I refilled our cups. "As Miss Evangeline's son, you are the heir to a whole lot more than Granger Mansion. The whole Carver estate should be yours."

"And do you realize what that means?" he asked. "It means I would have a pretty good motive for doing away with the estate's owner. I'm afraid, Ned, that birth certificate just makes me look guiltier than ever."

"There's something else," I said quietly. "The birth certificate is like a bull's-eye on your back. Miss Evangeline's cousins are expecting to inherit the estate. They believe they are the next of kin. Now, whether one of them is a murderer or not, when they find out you are her son, they might be quite willing to take out the competition—you."

"And that's why I'm asking you to keep this news to yourself," Ken said. "I'll show the birth certificate to Cade, but I don't want him or his sidekick to make it general knowledge."

I nodded. "That's the best. At least, for now."

Chapter 33

I wanted to talk to my mother. Or my husband Sloan. I had promised Ken I'd keep his secret, so I couldn't tell Pat or Jackie about him. I didn't want to discuss him with Cade because Cade had never liked Ken in the first place and would be doubly suspicious of him now. I couldn't even go next door to Miss Ann's because this astounding news, that Ken was Uncle Javin's son, must not be common knowledge, at least for a while. So, I drove to the old house place in town, the one I had shared with Mom and Dad until we left Ednalee for Atlanta.

The house was gone, but the sidewalk and the steps were still there. The oak tree in the back yard was there too.

The sun played hide and seek with the clouds, casting flitting shadows across the overgrown lawn as I got out of my car and walked to the back. Amazingly, remnants of my old rope swing still clung to a sturdy limb of the oak. The rope was frayed and gray, looking like it would disintegrate with the next strong breeze. I smiled, remembering the feel of the wind on my face as I flew through the air, higher and higher, up to the branches of the tree. How wonderful to be that carefree once again, to know nothing of grown-ups and their frailties.

Who owned this place now? Dad had sold it when we left. Why did the previous owner tear the house down? Why did he or she just let the whole thing fall into such disrepair?

Maybe I could buy it. Maybe I could rebuild the house. Perhaps I could rent it or just have it for a place to be when I felt as I did today—lonely and sad. Or, was that a frivolous thought, was I simply trying to hang onto the past when the past was gone? I hated to see this area neglected when it had been the home of the two dearest people in the world to me. I would talk to Daisy. Maybe she knew who it belonged to and if they might be willing to sell.

Wandering back to my car, I saw something half buried in the ground. Stooping down, I picked it up. A penny! And face up! I remembered an old saying from my childhood: *Find a penny, pick it up. All the day you'll have good luck.* Tucking it into my pocket, I smiled. It had been good to be here. Already, I felt better, more hopeful. I planned to talk to Daisy right away.

A movement caught my eyes and I glanced up. A figure stepped out from behind my car. My heart turned over and my breath caught in my throat. Moe Decker! Immediately, I was mindful of the loneliness of the place. The street had always been a quiet one, and we had owned a couple of acres. The house was the last one on the block, tucked back among a grove of trees. No one was around. On the whole street, it was only Moe Decker and me.

He grinned—not a friendly smile, but more of a grimace.

"So, we meet again, do we? And, it's a nice, cozy little meeting—just you and me. Enjoying the day, are you?" he asked.

Swallowing my panic, I gulped. "What are you doing here? How did you know where I was? Are you following me?"

He laughed. "Well now, why would you think that? Guilty conscience, maybe? I reckon it's a free country and I got as much right to be here as you have. Just thought I'd say howdy and inquire about that dog you stole from old Rawl."

I took a step back as he advanced toward me. "I didn't steal anything from Rawl. He was mean to Ulysses and I offered him food and a bed. Ulysses has a good home."

His eyes narrowed. "That's a lie. But then, I've heard you have a few problems of your own now. Been sticking your nose in again where it doesn't belong, haven't you? Just can't keep out of other people's business, can you? Maybe I'd just better teach you a lesson."

I knew that if I pressed my phone button for help, he would probably reach me before that help came. So, I'd try to bluff him.

Walking backward, I pulled my phone from its holster. "If you come any nearer, I'll press this button. It's programmed to 9-1-1. You're a jailbreaker and a criminal. I imagine the police chief will be glad to find you."

He paused, eying my upraised phone, probably trying to decide if he could reach me before I pressed the button.

"You win for now," he snarled. "But, just remember, lady, you'd better watch your back. You don't know where I'll be or when, and Moe Decker don't forget them who do him wrong."

Turning on his heel, he slunk across the street and disappeared into the bushes. I pressed the button on my phone anyway. I would report him and hope the law would find him and put him away. This time, for good.

Chapter 34

"At least, go next door to Miss Ann's house to spend the night," Cade pleaded.

We were sitting together on my sofa, watching the embers dying in the fireplace. Another chilly day. Would spring never arrive? My hand felt warm and secure within Cade's and I would have liked for the moment to go on and on, but I broke the spell.

Drawing a deep breath, I shook my head. "As much as I love Miss Ann, I can't take my animals to her house every night. They would be confused and uncomfortable. And I don't want to leave them in the house alone either. Don't worry, Cade. Ulysses is an excellent watchdog."

I almost wished I hadn't reported the Moe incident. All my friends, including Cade, were beginning to hover. Not that I wasn't grateful and not that I wasn't a bit apprehensive. I just didn't want to change my routine because of threats or possible danger. Every time anyone set foot inside a car, she courted danger. Life in these times was fraught with uncertainty, and there was no escaping the fact that we all should be mindful of possibilities. Besides, I certainly didn't feel the need for a bodyguard or a babysitter.

"I knew you wouldn't agree," Cade said. "Would you like me to take up residence here on your sofa each night?"

I grinned. "Now that would give wagging tongues in Ednalee something to talk about, wouldn't it? I'd love for you to be here, Cade, but your hours are so erratic that you're never sure when your day will end. Thanks, but no."

"No use telling you to be careful," he said. "Just keep your phone with you and don't hesitate to call. You still have that holster I gave you, don't you?"

I showed him the pretty blue leather phone holster clipped to the waistband of my jeans. "Sure do. And my phone is securely inside. I'll make a deal. I'll be careful, and you promise not to worry. Okay?"

He snorted. "Yeah, right."

"What about Ken? Where is he? I was floored when he handed me his birth certificate. To think, I actually have a cousin and I thought Uncle Javin was the last of my family."

Cade shook his head. "What a mix-up. It would have saved a lot of trouble if Miss Evangeline hadn't tried to keep him a secret all these years. And your uncle . . . well, I guess people have always been the same, past generations or today. But, it doesn't do any good to think of the 'if onlys.' Life has always had its mix-ups and surprises."

I quoted Walter Scott. "*Oh, what a tangled web we weave when first we practice to deceive.*" Why on earth were these things I learned in childhood coming back to me? Was it a form of comfort? Was I reverting to the time in my life when I felt safe with my parents? Could it be a sign of approaching old age?

"Exactly," Cade said. "I have Ken in protective custody for now. We don't know as yet who this killer is we're dealing with. It seems strange that the murders happened at the same time Moe escaped from jail, but why would he bother? Moe is as mean as they come, but so far, he hasn't resorted to murder. No, the person who would have the most to gain from murder would be one of the people at the Carver farm."

"Maybe it's somebody we haven't thought of yet," I said. "Maybe it's a person we would least suspect."

"Got any suggestions?" he asked.

I thought for a minute. "No, not right now."

"Can I borrow Ulysses for a while?" he asked.

"What? Ulysses? Why?"

"He's pretty good at trailing people, as I remember. If I took him out to your folks' old house place and let him sniff around, he might be able to pick up Moe's scent."

"He might," I agreed. "Sure, Cade, if you can keep up with him. If he runs off from you and finds Moe when he's alone, I think Moe would kill him."

Cade squeezed my hand. "I'll have him on a leash. That won't happen, I promise. I can come by after him first thing in the morning."

So, I agreed. I just didn't want any harm to come to my dog. He and Penny meant a great deal to me.

As Cade left, I turned to Ulysses. "Well, old friend, it looks like you are joining the police force for a while. Maybe tomorrow will put a period to at least one of our suspects."

But life, being full of quirks and twists, had another trick up its sleeve, because the next day, it rained.

Chapter 35

Nerves are treacherous, uncomfortable things. My nerves wouldn't let me settle down to read or watch television, and I didn't care to bake. So, I paced. Sometimes I got like this—just a strong, bad feeling that all was not well, that somewhere something was about to happen, and it would not be good. Although rain was usually one of my favorite sounds, today it was just a sporadic, monotonous, irritating dripping. Had there ever been such a rainy month?

Cade had come by early for Ulysses. As he left, he cautioned me again to stay inside the house, to keep doors and windows locked, and to have my cell phone at the ready. Although Cade assured me he would have Ulysses back before dark, I had gotten so used to having him in the house, talking to him, depending on him to bark a warning if someone came to the door, that the house seemed mighty vacant without him.

The events of the past couple of weeks alarmed and depressed me: three deaths, and even though finding an actual relative when I thought my family was all gone was a happy event, it still took a toll on my emotions. I worried about Cade and Gerald in their dangerous jobs and, well, let's face it—I was uncomfortable over my part in the situation with Miss Evangeline's will, or lack of it. I felt it my duty to ferret out her murderer. Had the same person killed Myra and Lila, or did we have two murderers to worry about?

Penny seemed to catch my mood. She paced over to the window, stiff-legged, hopped up on the back of the sofa, and stared out at the dismal day. Dark, menacing clouds hung low over Ednalee. Would we ever have sunny days again? Maybe Pat was right—maybe a blue moon month influenced the weather and people's moods. Maybe it turned ordinarily nice people into crazed killers.

Mentally, I shook myself and spoke aloud. "Stop it, Nettie Elizabeth! You are becoming as superstitious as Pat." I wouldn't give in to fear. What had happened to my faith?

A brilliant flash of lightning shivered through the room followed by a crack of thunder. I jumped and Penny disappeared upstairs, undoubtedly to crouch under my bed. The monotonous dripping became a roar as rain fell in torrents.

Where were Cade and Ulysses? Had my dog been able to pick up Moe's scent? Had they tracked him down? What if they cornered him and Moe shot them both?

Pouring a cup of coffee with hands that shook, I willed the phone to ring. I walked to the window and peered through the gray curtain of rain, hoping to see the glimmer of Cade's truck lights coming up the long driveway.

"Get hold of yourself," I muttered. "Cade is an experienced lawman. He won't do anything foolish and he will look out for Ulysses."

Knowing the rain would wash away all the scent from Moe's trail, I reassured myself by reasoning that Cade and Ulysses would soon give up the tracking mission as hopeless. They would come home, and all would be well.

I went through the entire house, flicking light switches in every room, even the bathroom. Hopefully, the electricity would stay on. Usually, I enjoyed being alone in this big old house, although it was better with Ulysses in it. But I drew the line at being alone in a big, old, dark house. If I called Miss Ann or Pat or Jackie, they would offer to come and stay with me, but I didn't want to ask them to come out in such a deluge.

I clicked on the light in the tiny room upstairs that I called my office and glanced at my computer. My camera lay beside it. It was not the smartest thing to turn on the computer during a storm, but this was not an ordinary day. At least, the computer would offer some sort of contact with other people. It was attached to a backup box, so it should be safe to use.

Realizing I hadn't downloaded my last few pictures, I scooted into my office chair and plugged my camera into an empty port. Within a few seconds, the latest images popped up. I scrolled through pictures of Ulysses and Penny and one of the Carver mansion.

A shiver ran through me as I gazed at this historic building. I had snapped the photo on the night Jackie, Pat, and I arrived at the farm, the night Miss Evangeline was found dead. Setting rays of the sun lay across part of the roof and lit the windows on the west side of the house. Its shadow stretched across the lawn. The trees around it were dark silhouettes, reaching with long, leafless branches toward the darkening sky.

Shivering, I scrolled to the next picture. Maybe it was the knowledge of what would be discovered only a short time after making the picture that caused the mansion to look ominous and, as Pat said, spooky.

The clump of cedars near the spot Miss Evangeline died filled the screen. I had snapped the photo as Ken and I were riding back to the barn. Enlarged, the picture showed more than I noticed with my naked eye—rocks, scuffed up dirt, briars, bushes, and trunks of scrub cedars. I leaned closer to the screen. What was that under a bush? Enlarging the picture further, I squinted, then got my magnifying glass. Something was out of place. A remnant of white hung from a low branch of a cedar. It looked like a piece of cloth and was entirely out of place in this area of rocks and trees.

I didn't have to glance out the window to know the storm was still going full blast. Thunder rumbled, lightning flashed, and here in this upstairs room, the rain sounded like a drum against the roof, but I wanted to know if that scrap of material was still there, attached to the prickly bush.

Penny crawled out from under the bed and jumped up on my lap.

"I'm so glad you decided to join me," I said, stroking her silky head. "You wouldn't think I was crazy for going out in this storm, would you?"

Her eyes darkened and she asked, "Prrt?"

"You're right. I shouldn't be so foolish," I said. "But, as soon as the storm lets up, I'm going back to the Carver farm. Surely, no one else will be out and about on such a soggy day. Cade told me to stay indoors, but did I agree? I don't think so."

Penny looked up at me and tapped my chin with one small paw. If she could have spoken, I felt sure she would have said that my idea was a dumb one and I should just show Cade the picture and let him check to see if the object was still there. The wind might have blown it away by now.

With one last reproachful look, Penny hopped off my knees and trotted out of the bedroom door, legs stiff and tail pointing up. If I phoned Cade, he would tell me not to go, and Pat and Jackie would think I was probably on a fool's errand. That's why I would make sure they didn't. Know, that is.

To fill in the time until the rain decided to go away, I would do some computer searches. Typing in the names of Miss Evangeline's kinfolk might net some interesting results. It was only a chance, but anything gleaned about that family should be useful.

First, I typed in Elbert Carver. A few results came up, none of them meaningful until I opened the last one. A mental light bulb blinked on. Elbert had not come to the Carver farm to help Miss Evangeline. He came because he had nowhere else to go. Due to some poor business decisions and a shady deal or two, Elbert was bankrupt. He had lost his home, his savings, even his job. In light of all this, it would be fair to say that Elbert was desperate. He needed money badly, but did he need it badly enough to murder for it?

Next was Elbert's wife Pearly. She had been involved in a lawsuit at about the same time Elbert declared bankruptcy. The suit was brought by an enterprise that had a chain of casinos. What had happened? How interesting. Cade had mentioned that Pearly's brother who actually wasn't a brother, Mick Morrow, worked for a gambling establishment. Surely there was a connection. Pearly would have been at the farm because Elbert was there, but why was Mick there too?

I typed in Veda Johnson. Scrolling through, I could find nothing on her. It was as if she did not exist. Why? Was this her real name? Why wasn't there even a mention, however small?

A leaf shadow fell across my computer and I looked out of the window. The sun was out! The rain had stopped, however temporarily. If I was going to go to the Carver farm and try to find that bush in my picture and retrieve the scrap, now was the time!

Chapter 36

I grabbed my raincoat just in case the clouds decided to open up again, pulled on my rain boots because I knew the grass would be squishy, found my umbrella and purse, and headed for my car which was parked under the carport. Rain dripped from tree branches as I started down my driveway. I switched on the windshield wipers for a few minutes, splatted through puddles, and soon reached the road out of town toward the Carver estate.

I was so busy suppressing my bossy inner voice that kept insisting I was doing a foolish thing, that I nearly missed the turnoff to the farm. Seeing it at the last minute, I wrenched my steering wheel to the right and crept down the flooded lane toward the mansion.

How would I know when I had reached the part of the pasture where Miss Evangeline had met her death? I tried to estimate how far Ken and I had ridden that morning. It seemed to me the clump of cedars would have been directly west of this road, but between the road and the pasture was a heavy stand of trees, very wet, dripping trees, which looked amazingly like the trees lining the path from Myra's house to the mansion. Although I didn't admit it to many people, I was directionally challenged. Besides, to me, trees were all oaks or maples. It was not beyond the realm of possibility that if I tried to find my way through these woods, I would get lost.

Hopefully, the clouds and early twilight would conceal my movements from anybody in the house. Having discarded the idea of trying to walk through the thick grove of trees, I drove my car onto the shoulder of the road and pondered the problem. Ken was no longer in residence, so I couldn't ask his advice. Cade said he was in protective custody. He and I had ridden into the pasture from the barn, the day we found the spot where Miss Evangeline had died. With the barn as my starting point, surely I could find the cedar thicket and that intriguing bit of white caught on a low limb.

I slung my purse over my shoulder and opened the car door. A gust of wind nearly pushed me back inside the cab. What was I thinking, coming alone to a place where murder had happened? A little voice inside my head kept repeating, *Fool's errand, fool's errand.*

Struggling against the wind, I concentrated on finding the barn. At last, the mansion rose through the shadows. Dodging away from those long windows, I crept behind hedges and trees until, at last, I reached the barn.

I squinted into the pasture, trying to get my bearings. Finally, I crossed my fingers and started in the general direction Ken and I had ridden.

After what seemed an eon of battling the wind, I stumbled over a rock and glanced down at my feet. A good sign! I remembered that rocks littered the area where Miss Evangeline's ride had ended. Soon a clump of cedars that looked familiar rose from the pasture. My heart quickened. I had found it!

I dropped to my knees within the thicket. The photo had shown the white object nearly obscured by low-hanging branches, only inches from the ground. Rummaging in my purse, I found a small flashlight and shone its thin beam around the area. The wet grass soaked my jeans as I crawled from cedar to cedar.

At last, my light picked out that intriguing white scrap. Carefully unwinding it from a stubby limb, I smoothed it out over my knee. It was a piece of linen, and, even though it was muddy and bedraggled, I could tell it had been torn from something larger, something like a tablecloth or maybe a sheet. An embroidered letter near the hem, a fancy letter C, identified it as belonging to the estate. What would an article from the linen closet of the mansion be doing out here in the pasture, caught on a low-hanging limb, very near the spot where Miss Evangeline had died?

Standing up, I stuffed the remnant into my purse. This could be important. It might have a bearing on the way Miss Evangeline died, although at the moment I couldn't see a relationship. I would share my discovery with Cade. Maybe he could determine its importance.

A cold prickle of fear ran down my back as I felt, rather than saw, a presence behind me. I heard a footstep and a breath—I was not alone. Before I could turn around, something crashed against my skull. A thousand lights exploded before my eyes, and blackness closed around me.

Chapter 37

The beat, beat of a hammer jarred me awake. It took a few seconds to realize that the constant rhythmic pounding was my pulse throbbing against my eardrums. For a few minutes, I lay still, hoping the pain would subside. I was cold and wet which, evidently, came from lying on the ground, not in my bed, but why was I not there?

Finally, with a great effort, I opened my eyes as memory seeped back. The last place I remembered was the Carver estate. Now, I lay across rocks and soggy grass and the pungent scent of cedars filled my nostrils. I was cold all the way to my very bones, and, because I was on my stomach, the bottoms of cedars and rocks were all I could see.

I tried to stop shivering and remember what had happened. With a great effort, I flopped onto my back. The branches of a tree rose above me and beyond that, a few high-flying clouds covered and uncovered the face of the moon. It was not quite dark, just somewhere between sunset and night, the time of day that my grandparents would have called the *gloaming*.

Slowly, I sat up, holding my head with both hands to keep it from exploding. My fingers touched a sizable knot on the back of my head, and I closed my eyes until a wave of nausea and pain passed. Pushing myself to my feet, I stood, wobbling, but at least I was standing. The last thing I remembered was a noise behind me. Someone must have crept up and hit me on the head with something hard and unforgiving. Why had my attacker not killed me while I lay helpless?

Remembering the reason I had come on this mission, I glanced at my purse, lying open on the ground. I bent cautiously, picked it up, and looked inside. I probed the corners, checking every pocket, but there was no bit of white cloth anywhere. If someone had nearly killed me to get that remnant of material, it must be important. Did the person who had done this think I was actually dead? My head felt as if it had been a close call. The fact that I was only a few feet from the spot where Miss Evangeline had died was not lost on me.

Each movement jarred my head as I tried to retrace my route. Closing my lips against the pain, I hurried, lest my attacker still lurked and was, perhaps, watching. I had to get out of here. Besides, if Cade returned Ulysses and found me gone, he'd start a search party. How would I explain setting out by myself to the scene of a crime to find a small scrap of material? It sounded crazy, even to me.

At last, I reached the barn. I glanced toward the mansion. Lights glowed from the downstairs windows. How friendly and welcoming they seemed! Deceitfully so, because surely it was someone within those walls who had followed me and knocked me unconscious. But who? Was it just one person or was the whole Carver clan in some sort of conspiracy to get rid of everyone who stood between them and an inheritance? I was grateful that I had not become victim number four—at least, not yet.

Hoping no one within the house chanced to peer out of a window, I scurried up the road until I reached my car. I fumbled in my purse for the key, unlocked the door, and more or less fell inside.

I rubbed my eyes to clear them of a film that threatened my vision, jabbed my key into the ignition, started the engine, turned around, and pointed my SUV back toward Ednalee. I would not feel safe until I was inside my house.

Darkness had truly fallen by the time my driveway came in sight. Lights shone from the carriage house. I breathed a blessing on Coradee and Gerald, asking the Lord to keep them safe from

Coradee's evil uncle. Had Moe been the one who knocked me out? Had Ulysses been able to find him?

My yard looked as if somebody was having a party. Lights blazed from every window. Pat's and Jackie's cars, Cade's truck, and Gerald's car were parked in the driveway. All hope of sneaking back home and keeping quiet until I could think about my escapade and decide who I wanted to tell, and how much, flew out the window. Evidently, Cade had returned Ulysses, found me gone, and rounded up a posse.

Chapter 38

Cade had left a full pot of coffee for me the next morning. Grateful, I poured a cup, found his note, and sank into a dining chair. I rubbed my blurry eyes and read, *Please stay inside. The doctor said you shouldn't move around much. I'll call later.*

Ulysses laid his head on my knee and I reached down to smooth his silky ears. What a night! When the crowd that gathered here last night, consisting of Cade, Gerald, Coradee, Miss Ann, Pat, and Jackie, saw my disheveled and muddy state, to say nothing of the lump on my head, they carted me off to the emergency room. So, I now wore a bandage under my hair and was fortified with pain pills and directions from a stern Dr. Ghormley that I must stay inside, eat lightly, and rest. He would get no argument from me. Every bone in my body ached, as did my head. And I had about as much strength as Penny. Plus, lying out on the wet ground had brought on a cold. All in all, I felt miserable.

Since I refused to spend the night in the hospital for observation, Cade had slept on my sofa to keep an eye on me. I was grateful for his concern, but today I was even more grateful to just be left alone so I could be miserable in private and not have to talk to anybody.

No need for all those warnings from my friends about staying in-doors, not opening the door unless I trusted the person on the porch, and being wary of unknown callers on the phone. I agreed with it all. I was through with being brave and foolhardy. I could have been killed last night. Why wasn't I? If the person who caused this awful headache and achy cold was the same one who had killed three times before, why didn't he snuff me out too?

Sneezing, I poured another cup of coffee and took it and the afghan to the sofa. I just wanted to sleep. I didn't want to think about murderers or scraps of material hiding under bushes or wills or greedy relatives.

The coffee relaxed me, contrary to what caffeine is supposed to do, and the afghan felt warm around my shoulders. Penny snuggled against me and Ulysses crowded in beside us. I set my empty cup on the floor, scooted lower under the warmth of the afghan, and slept.

I dreamed I smelled potato soup. When I opened my eyes, Miss Ann stood at the kitchen stove, stirring a pot of the actual stuff. She turned and smiled at me as I sat up.

"That smells wonderful," I muttered, stifling a yawn. "How long have you been here?"

"Since a few minutes ago," she said. "I have a key, you know. Do you feel like eating just a bit? Nothing like good old potato soup to put strength in a body."

I smiled and threw back the afghan, dislodging Penny. Ulysses had deserted me in favor of looking hopefully up at the soup.

"Yes, thanks. There's really no need for you to mess up your day by babysitting me, although I certainly appreciate your being here. I'm feeling much better."

I stood up, waiting until the room stopped spinning to walk toward the table.

Miss Ann shook her head and spooned the thick soup into a bowl. "There's no place I'd rather be. I'll stay until Pat and Jackie get here. And they'll stay until Cade comes around again tonight."

Tears stung my eyes. Did anyone ever have such wonderful friends?

"Now, that's ridiculous," I said and grabbed a napkin to cover my sneeze. "I'll be fine by myself. Ulysses will be here to guard the house, and I'm really not an invalid."

Miss Ann frowned at me. "You have a concussion, plus the fact that someone nearly killed you. You're just lucky you have such a hard head."

I took a deep breath. "You're right. My guardian angel is working overtime."

"He gets no rest at all," Miss Ann said, putting the bowl of soup and a glass of tea on the table.

"Fill a bowl for yourself," I insisted.

She shook her head. "I ate a bite before coming and I'm not hungry. How are you feeling?"

"Like someone conked me on the head and I lay on the wet ground for hours," I said, taking a spoonful of the soup. "This is delicious."

"I wonder if whoever hit you thought he had killed you," Miss Ann mused, sinking into a chair opposite mine.

I shuddered. "Maybe. Maybe something scared him off before he could finish the job."

"Oh, Nettie, I do wish you weren't so . . . so inquisitive," she said.

I grinned. "You were going to say nosy, weren't you?"

She nodded. "Well, yes, as a matter of fact, I was."

The hot soup plus Miss Ann's concern did a lot to make me feel better. Wrapping the shawl around my shoulders, I walked back to the sofa.

"Come sit down and talk to me," I invited. "I guess I don't want to be alone after all."

She smiled. "That's good, because I see Pat and Jackie have just arrived."

She went to the door to let them in and then poured more tea. We all sat around the fireplace, which didn't contain a fire but seemed to add a certain cozy feel to the room.

"Okay," Pat said, "spill it, Sherlock. You mumbled something last night about trying to find a scrap of somebody's tablecloth. I must not have understood because that doesn't sound like much to risk getting killed."

Jackie frowned. "Don't be hard on her. She doesn't feel all that well. Her eyes are bloodshot and I'm sure her head is throbbing."

"It's all right. I'll feel better if I talk about it," I said.

So, I told my three closest friends about sighting the cloth in a picture I'd taken of the Carver farm, about the trip to the estate, finding the scrap, then losing it. And the longer I talked, the more I realized what a foolish thing I'd done.

My eyes started to water as I said, "But the thing I'm sorriest about is causing worry to the people I love best in all the world. And now, look at you all! You've given up a good part of your day to stay with your wayward friend. I'm so sorry!"

Miss Ann went to the bathroom, brought back a box of tissues, and handed it to me.

"Give me one," Pat said, tears running down her face.

Jackie grabbed a tissue as Miss Ann passed it around then sat down on the sofa beside me. We were all four squeezed together, but it felt good.

"If we aren't the beatinest!" Miss Ann said. "Why are we crying, anyway? We're all safe. The Lord kept Nettie alive, and I realize how blessed I am to have you girls in my life. We should be on top of the world."

Pat blew her nose and giggled. "Girls? It has been a long time since someone called me a girl, like, maybe thirty years ago."

"I know what you're saying, Miss Ann. But, you know, I don't think Ned or any of us will be truly safe until whoever is running around the county killing people is caught and put away for life," Jackie said.

I nodded. "That's true. But I'm going to behave and leave it up to Cade and Gerald and the sheriff and whoever else is working on this. I'm through with playing detective! Done! I'm going to settle in with my animals and think about giving a shower for Coradee and live a quiet life. Starting now!"

I tried not to see the looks of disbelief on the faces of my friends. And I ignored that niggling little flame of curiosity that, try as I might, wouldn't quite be quenched.

That silly scrap of cloth probably had a perfectly innocent reason to be out in the middle of the pasture caught on a bush a few feet from where a murder had taken place. I would put it out of my mind.

However, I felt sure it was important. I just didn't know how or why. When my head quit hurting, maybe the answer would come to me. Maybe it would be like that little light bulb in cartoons that illustrated a bright idea. But, of course, if the answer popped into my head, I'd just tell Cade about it. That would be the sensible thing to do, wouldn't it?

Chapter 39

I assured Cade the next morning that I wouldn't need a bodyguard any longer. He wasn't happy about it, but I made him understand that I would be extra cautious, I had his number on speed dial, and I was feeling guilty about the sleep he was losing. After all, sleeping on my sofa long term couldn't be all that comfortable.

"Was Ulysses able to track Moe?" I asked. "Is he locked away again?"

Cade shook his head. "No, Ulysses found his scent at your old house place and followed it into the woods, but then the rain started pouring and he lost it."

"So, it could have been Moe who slugged me?"

Cade nodded, his face grim. "It could have been, Ned."

"Well, I'm here. I'm alive and I'll be fine by myself. I promise. Please go back to work and don't worry about me."

He didn't look convinced, but he left, and my conscience eased some.

Jackie, Miss Ann, and Pat were next on my list. I called them and told them that although I loved them dearly, I really needed some time alone to sort out a few things, and they should continue with their lives, without further disruption by taking care of me.

Feeling not quite as confident as I made my friends believe, I settled down with a paper and pencil to see if I could make sense of the happenings of the last few days. Writing my thoughts on paper helped, but as yet, I hadn't succeeded in doing that.

With my full cup of coffee before me, I perched on a chair at the dining table and prepared to do some logical thinking. That's when the phone rang.

I listened for the third ring and the answering machine to take over. I would swear that the low, guttural voice was the same one who had called before I went to Myra's house, the night I found her dead in the maze.

"Mrs. McNeil," said the voice, "you were warned to stay out of things that don't concern you. Next time, you won't be so lucky. You will get more than a knot on your head if you don't back off."

The phone clicked and the call ended. I shivered as a chill ran over me. Another warning. Who? The murderer, I'd bet, but who? He or she evidently knew my telephone number. Should I change it? Did he know where I lived? Should I call Cade? Should I check into a motel or go to Miss Ann's for the night?

Taking a few deep breaths to try to slow my pounding heart, I resolutely picked up my pencil again. It was hard to collect my thoughts. The wound on the back of my head began to throb. Closing my eyes, I formed a silent prayer, asking the Lord for help. What should I do? It was hard to combat evil directed at me from an unknown source, and it was hard to think of anything else.

How had I gotten involved in this situation? Was I really meddling? I had decided to trust the police to handle the murder investigations, but how was I supposed to let the threatening caller know this? I just wished the whole investigation was finished and the killer caught and made to pay for his crimes. If only Miss Evangeline hadn't called me to take those pictures. If only she hadn't told me she suspected someone was trying to kill her. But, she had done both those things. I just wished I didn't feel an obligation to find her killer, because I had decided to stay out of the investigation.

Putting my pencil down, I went to the phone. I would call Cade. I lifted the receiver, then hesitated. What could he do that I couldn't?

149

I could change my own phone number. I could use call blocker, although that didn't always work for me. Instead of calling Cade, I called the phone company. I'd try call blocker first. And as for telling Cade about it, what would that do, other than cause him to worry?

After changing my calling plan with the phone company, I exchanged my cold coffee for a fresh, hot cup and sat down again. I would be in danger until the murderer/anonymous caller was caught. If I could come up with a serious suspect, I'd tell Cade and that would be the end of my involvement.

At the top of a clean sheet of paper, I wrote, "Motives." That was easy. Money. Lots and lots of money. That might have prompted any of Miss Evangeline's relatives to resort to that vilest of all crimes. Next, I wrote "Opportunity." That, too, was easy. Who would have a better opportunity than the cousins she had taken in? Pearly and Elbert lived on the estate, as did Veda. Veda was an unknown. I could find no information about her on the internet.

Although I hated to entertain the idea, there were Jules and Ken. How hard would it have been for any of these people to somehow cause Melanie to bolt and then hit her frail rider on the head as she lay, disabled, on the ground?

That brought up another question. Had forensics decided exactly what the murderer had used to hit Miss Evangeline?

Mick Morrow—I added him to my list of suspects. I didn't think he had been at the Carver farm when Miss Evangeline died, but did I know for sure? If he and Pearly had the idea of turning the estate into a gambling establishment, he'd have plenty of motive for getting rid of any obstacles in their path, including the owner of the estate.

Shrugging, I listed Tyler, Ken's helper, and the list of unknown workers about the place. But, what would their motives be? How would they benefit from the death of an employer who, people said, treated them well?

Moe was a suspect, but who else should be on my list, besides those living or working there? I'd never heard that Miss Evangeline attended church, and I had no way of knowing what other activities she might have been involved with or what people she had known.

Next came the question, What had Myra and Lila known that resulted in their deaths? The timing of Miss Evangeline's murder seemed plain. She was going to see a lawyer to make out a will. She had to die before she accomplished that.

If only Miss Evangeline had made a will years ago. Ron said that her father had made a trust. If he'd made such a document and the lawyer's copy had been destroyed in a fire, where was the copy belonging to old Judson? Was it hidden in the mansion? Could it be behind the loose brick in the fireplace? If it was there, how would I ever manage to get back inside and find out? Then, I brought myself up short. I wouldn't. I had bowed out of the situation.

Swallowing the last drop of coffee in my cup, I probed the bump on the back of my head. The scrap of cloth caught under a bush—why was it so important that someone knocked me unconscious to get it? I felt it was the key to the murder.

"What do you think about this whole thing?" I asked Ulysses, who was sleeping at my feet. "And how can I just walk away and forget it? Oh, I know that I promised Cade and myself and everyone else that I would stay home and be sensible, and I'll try, so if I come up with any answers, I'll pass them along to him."

Ulysses perked up, jumped to his feet, looked at me questioningly, and trotted toward the door.

I was wondering whether he was trying to answer my questions when I heard a car in the driveway. Glancing out the window, I saw an older brown sedan stop, then a few seconds later, Jules Thatcher walked toward my porch.

Chapter 40

My friends' cautions rang in my ears. I had promised not to open the door to someone I didn't know, but I knew Jules Thatcher. He may have saved my life that night in the maze. Besides, any person who got so involved in reading his favorite books that he took on the persona of the characters could surely be trusted. Pushing aside the fact that I had just added his name to my list of suspects, I opened the door and invited him inside.

"I came to say goodbye, Miss Ned," Jules said as he and I sat in the living room. I had poured coffee for both of us, and now he turned his mug around and around, gazing at the dark liquid.

"Oh? Are you going on a trip?" I asked, noting that today he seemed to be himself, just Jules Thatcher and not a fictional character.

He sighed. "You might say so. A mighty long one. I'm leaving Ednalee, leaving Oklahoma. I need to get far, far away from that bunch who've taken over Miss Evangeline's home."

"I'm sorry to hear that," I said. "Why are you going?" I didn't mention it to Jules, but I wondered if the sheriff would approve of his leaving and if it would be considered suspicious.

Jules finished half his coffee before he answered. "I hate to admit this, but I'm scared. I don't trust anybody that's left out there on the farm. Those relatives of Miss Eva's—if they are really relatives and aren't just liars—are a sneaky bunch. I think one of them is responsible for her death. And I'm afraid they're suspicious of me. They think maybe I know something about why those three women died. And maybe I do."

My pulse quickened. This man, looking intently at me, was a troubled soul. Real fear flickered in his green eyes.

"Jules," I said softly, "do you want to share what you know with me?"

Setting his mug on the floor, he clasped his hands together between his knees and leaned toward me.

"After I tell you what I know and what I suspect, I'm going to disappear. I thought maybe somebody else besides me should know, just in case something happens to me and I don't make my getaway. I guess you know this, Miss Ned, you are in danger. The Carver kin don't like the fact that you're snooping around. I heard them arguing about you one night."

My lips felt tight as I asked, "You heard them mention me?"

He nodded. "I was supposed to have gone home, it was past quittin' time, but there were some spring plantings I wanted to get in, some shrubs to replace the ones that had died during the winter. They didn't know I was right under the window, and I heard Pearly yelling at Elbert.

"'I don't like it a bit,' she said. 'That McNeil woman is snooping around, I tell you. I wouldn't trust her as far as I could throw her.'"

I rubbed my arms which were suddenly cold. "Is that all you heard?"

"That's about it," Jules said. "But I catch them throwing me sidelong glances. It's an unhappy house out there now, an uneasy house. I'm afraid that what happened to Myra might happen to me. And you, Miss Ned, you've got to be careful. Maybe you should get out of town too."

I got up and started pacing. The fight or flight syndrome had struck me full force. I couldn't sit still.

"What else makes you uneasy?" I asked, pausing by my chair. "You knew both Myra and Lila, didn't you? You had worked on the farm for quite a while."

Jules motioned toward the chair. "Please sit down, Miss Ned, or I'll feel like I should stand up too and, frankly, I'm tired. Feel like I've got a weight on my shoulders."

I sat on the edge of my chair. "I need to know your thoughts, Jules," I said. "You've told me this much. Tell me the rest of what you know."

He leaned back, ran his hand over his stubble of a beard, and gazed at the ceiling.

"Yes, I knew both Lila and Myra. Lila had been a housekeeper for Miss Eva for a long, long time. I believe Lila's mother and Miss Eva were girls together and were friends. There was never any doubt about Lila. She was trustworthy. She wouldn't ever have done anything to hurt Miss Eva. Lila and me—we were the only two on the place that Miss Eva trusted. You remember what she said that day at the grave-yard? She accused somebody of being a murderer. I think she must have heard or seen something that caused her to believe that. And I think whoever it was she accused killed her and hoped it'd be blamed on the storm."

I would never forget that day, the second death connected with the Carver farm. Lila had been a trusted employee, a friend to her em-ployer. I wondered if Miss Evangeline had told her, as she told me, that somebody was trying to kill her.

Jules scooted back and gripped his knees with his hands. He looked down at the floor, then up at me.

"Myra. I knew her when she was just a girl. Then, she grew up and got married. Old Judson Carver treated her and her husband awful, foreclosing on their home. Of course, he took our home too, but I got over the bitterness. I don't think Myra ever did. Miss Eva wasn't any-thing like her father. I think she actually hired us—Myra and me—to try and make up for some of old Jud's meanness."

I felt the need to pace again. Grabbing Jules's mug and my own, I took them to the coffee pot and refilled them.

"So, Myra was resentful of her boss? Do you think she tried to get even with her?" I asked, handing him the steaming mug.

"Maybe," Jules said, squinting through the steam. "I saw something kind of strange the day Miss Eva died, and it just stuck in my mind. It was around noontime. I was about to quit work and have lunch, thought I'd walk over to the stables and see if Ken or Tyler wanted to eat with me. I saw Myra coming back toward the house. She had come from the pasture, from the direction everybody said Miss Eva died. Myra had something white all rolled up in her hands and looked to me like she was scared. She was hurrying and kept looking behind her."

The coffee in my mouth suddenly tasted sour. I gulped and said, "She had something white in her hands?"

He nodded.

"Like a—like, maybe a tablecloth?" I whispered.

Jules shrugged. "I don't know. I suppose it could have been."

My mind whirled. Myra was still bitter toward Miss Evangeline. Myra, at the luncheon, had been upset and wanted to tell me something, but didn't want anyone else to hear. Myra's empty house, her body in the maze—she knew something about the murder, but what? Somehow, I couldn't picture Myra clubbing Miss Evangeline to death. I could, however, picture her hiding behind a bush in the pasture, white tablecloth in hand, a cloth she had taken from the Carver kitchen. I could imagine her stepping out from the bush, flapping the cloth, and startling Miss Evangeline's mare.

So, had she meant to give Miss Eva a good scare, make her little mare run? And then, when she saw Miss Eva on the ground and thought she was dead, she might have been scared. But what had she hoped to accomplish? What was the point? And, why would it have happened the day Miss Evangeline had planned to see a lawyer? Had Myra been the one lurking behind a corner the night I talked to Miss Eva?

Maybe Myra had meant to confess this to me. But, if she had, if she had meant only to confess what she had done, why would someone have killed her? No, she had meant to implicate someone else and that person didn't want that to happen, so Myra was killed.

"Miss Ned? Are you all right?" Jules's anxious voice interrupted my thoughts.

Taking a deep breath, I reached out and squeezed his hand. "Yes, yes, I'm fine, Jules. Thank you for coming. You've helped more than you know. I think you're right. You'd better get as far away from the Carver farm as you can. You're not safe here. I'm going to share with the chief of police what you've told me. He's working with the sheriff. Maybe, before too long, you'll be able to come back home."

Jules stood up and I walked him to the door. He stepped onto the porch and pointed at a potted bonsai tree beside the door.

"Miss Eva gave me that tree," he said. "It was on an evening after we'd shared a nightcap. She walked over to a plant stand and said, 'Jules, I want you to take care of this for me. It belonged to my father. I don't want it to die, and if anything should happen to me, who'd water it and take care of it?' So, of course, I took it home. Maybe she had a premonition that she wouldn't live much longer."

He shrugged. "Anyway, Miss Ned, I can't take it with me, and I can't leave it in my house. Nobody would water it. Will you take it?"

I was touched by his concern for Miss Eva's wishes. "Of course I will," I promised. "Be careful, Jules. Be suspicious of everyone. Whoever murdered three times won't hesitate to murder again."

Chapter 41

"Do you feel well enough to be out?" This was Cade's greeting when I walked into his office.

Assuring him that I certainly did, I told him about Jules's visit and the conversation we'd had. Then, I told him that I thought the scrap of white material caught on the cedar tree had come from a tablecloth and may have been the one Jules saw Myra with the day of Miss Evangeline's death.

Cade closed one eye and rubbed his mustache, a sure sign of deep thought. Finally, he shook his head.

"You may be right, Ned. That sure sounds suspicious. However, we've got four good suspects out at the Carver place, five, if I count Ken. Of course, he's tucked away out of sight right now. So, which one was it? Or, are they all in this together? Guess I ought to tell you, though, forensics identified the murder weapon that killed Miss Evangeline. It was a hammer."

I shuddered. "Oh, Cade! A hammer! Somebody hit that poor little woman with a hammer while she lay on the ground?"

"Looks that way," he said. "However, here comes the interesting part—it wasn't just any hammer. It was the kind farriers use when they shoe horses."

The bad feeling in the pit of my stomach grew. I didn't want to hear what he was going to say next.

"As you know, your newfound cousin shoes horses—he shod a lot of them for Miss Evangeline. You want to know where we found that hammer?"

I shook my head. "Not really."

"We found it in Ken's tool shed—the one where he kept the supplies for the horses. And the only fingerprints on it were Ken's."

I swallowed a couple of times before I could speak. "But, Cade, Ken was already in protective custody when I was attacked out in the Carver pasture."

"If he hadn't been, he'd be in a lot more trouble than he's in right now. As it is, looks like somebody may be trying to frame Ken. They could have worn gloves, and been careful how they handled the hammer that killed Miss Evangeline, and planted it back in the tool shed where Ken kept it."

"Do you happen to have any coffee that wasn't made yesterday?" I asked, looking around his office.

He grinned. "My feelings are hurt. The coffee in this office is always fresh and piping hot. One lovely Styrofoam cupful coming up."

The coffee, when Cade handed me a cup, was hot, and that was the main reason I had asked for it. It helped warm my cold hands. I took a small sip and felt it burn all the way down to my stomach.

"Whew!" I gasped. "No wonder you're able to work all day and half the night. This has enough caffeine to float a spoon."

Before he could answer, I went on. "Let's think about this. Why would any of the Carver family want to throw suspicion on Ken unless they know about his birth and are framing him to make sure he doesn't inherit? And how would they know that he is Miss Evangeline's son, since Miss Evangeline kept it a secret all these years and Ken himself didn't know until recently she was his mother?"

"I'd say the family knows, but I don't know how unless Myra or Lila knew and told them," he said. "And how'd Lila and Myra know? Or, maybe they just suspected as much."

I suddenly felt tired. Setting the coffee on his desk, I rose to my feet. "I'll leave it with you, Cade. I'm going home, feed my animals, put my feet up, and think about this. Maybe I'll get a sudden inspiration."

Cade walked to the door with me. He gathered me in his arms for a quick hug. "Lock your doors. I'll have a deputy keep watch until I can get there tonight. No. No arguments. I think you should put in an alarm system, Ned. Even Ulysses or I or any number of watchmen can sometimes slip up. I'll feel a lot better if you have electronic eyes surveilling your place twenty-four hours a day."

Although I didn't tell him, I was glad Cade would spend another night on my sofa. "I promise," I said. "Although you are a lot more company than some old electronic spy."

He grinned as I left. "See you tonight," he said.

Chapter 42

"I, for one, badly needed this," I said, sipping my cup of hot caramel mocha coffee.

Grandy's was a warm, relaxing place any time, but it was especially welcoming when a cold March wind rattled the leaves outside and clouds threatened more rain.

Pat grinned. "You needed what? The coffee or our priceless friendship?"

I grinned back. "Both, actually."

"So did I," said Jackie. "Remember I told you about Mike, the boy Ron is trying to help? Well, what would you think if I said we may be adding him to our family?"

I set my cup down with a clatter. "You're what? Do you mean you are planning to adopt him?"

Jackie nodded. "We're still in the thinking and talking phase. It's exciting and there's so much to work out and, oh, I am so scared!"

"It's a big step," I agreed. "Are you scared as in good scared or bad scared?"

Jackie gripped her coffee cup tightly. "Good and bad. Do we really know what we're doing? What a responsibility! But mostly, I'm just excited. He's a really sweet boy, but what do I know about children or being a mother?"

Pat reached across the table and patted Jackie's free hand. "You'll be a super mom. That's the best news I've heard since Gerald told me they're expecting."

My emotions were torn between being happy for my friend and feeling hurt that she hadn't told me adoption might be in the works. But, this wasn't about me. It was about Jackie and Ron and a little boy named Mike. "Super," I echoed. "It's wonderful, Jackie. I didn't know you were even considering it."

I looked up as Daisy scooted in beside me, holding a glass of Coke. "Considering what? Or, is it none of my business?"

Jackie repeated her announcement.

"Well," Daisy said, "if you'd care to hear my opinion, and I'm sure you don't, but, anyway, I think that's terrific. A child is just what you and Ron need to perk up your old age."

Jackie sputtered. "Old age? Pardon me?"

Daisy laughed. "I'm kidding. I'm just referring to the fact that you three call yourselves the Mature Mouseketeers."

I gigged her in the ribs. "That's *The Three Musketeers*, thank you."

Still smiling, Daisy said, "Kidding aside, I'm happy you've made that big decision to take a child into your lives." She turned toward me. "I do apologize for barging in, but when I saw you, Ned, I thought I'd give you the good news about your parents' old home place. I've talked to the owner and she's not only willing, she's eager to sell. I think I can negotiate a pretty good deal for you."

The day seemed suddenly brighter. "Say, Daisy, that's great."

"I thought you'd be glad," she said. "Maybe we can get together someday soon with the current owner and talk about the nitty-gritty, which would be price."

I was already forming plans about the land. Should I put up another house? Would I want to live there or rent it and what sort of structure should it be?

"You bet," I said. "The sooner the better. Thanks, Daisy."

"This seems to be the day for good things to happen," Pat said. "And you know what? It's about time! March is nearly gone and with it, that troublesome blue moon. Now, if the murderer who has been wreaking havoc on the Carver legacy would just step forward and confess."

"That's not likely to happen," Jackie said. "And, Ned, don't look on that as a challenge. Remember, you're supposed to be letting Cade and Sheriff Cordray handle it."

I finished my mocha and dabbed my mouth with a napkin. "That's just what I'm doing. In case I'm tempted to do otherwise, I have a small reminder to stay away from the Carver farm." I gingerly felt the knot on my head.

"Oops, I'd better be going," Daisy said, glancing at her watch. "I have a client to meet. That reminds me, would you believe that one of the Carvers, Pearly, came by the office and asked what sort of value I'd set on the farm?"

I sputtered as heat rose to my face. "She didn't!"

"Yes, she did," Daisy said, getting to her feet. "And I understand the place hasn't even gone to probate yet. Some eager beavers out there."

"Now, Ned," Pat said as I shrugged into my jacket. "Don't get a bee in your bonnet. Remember your promise. There's nothing you can do about the Carvers, one way or the other. Somebody out there, or maybe the whole clan, is devious and dangerous. They can't do a thing legally. Not yet, anyway."

I took a deep breath. "You're right. And I don't plan to do anything. I don't even know what I *could* do. I just wish the sheriff and Cade would hurry up and put the murderer in jail, whoever he or she is."

"Or, whoever *they* are," Jackie added. "Thing is, please watch your back."

Those were my exact intentions.

Chapter 43

Remembering my friends' admonitions to stay safe, I meandered downtown. What safer place to be than the city library? Libraries are wonderful sanctuaries any time as well as being storehouses of information. Added to those charms was the fact that the librarian, Greta, was a good friend of mine.

The library, as Grandy's, was a refuge from wild, windy weather such as we were experiencing today. I loved the smell that always greeted me when I opened the library's door. The elusive scent of books, papers, floor wax, and an indefinable something born of years. Could knowledge have its own aroma, an *essence of library*?

"Greta," I said, leaning across her desk, "I'm curious about the Carver family. All I know is hearsay and my short acquaintance with Miss Evangeline. Where could I look to find out more actual facts?"

Greta smiled. "They are an intriguing family, aren't they? Even though, from what I hear, Judson was as mean as the dickens. Still, he's rather shadowy. But it's my job to dispel those shadows! You'll be pleased to know that our reference department is blessed with Scan-Pro. We have all the old newspaper stories from Ednalee on microfilm. My advice would be to start there."

I felt like a prospector, excited about the possibility of discovering gold. "Oh, great!" I said, rubbing my hands together. "Show me the way."

Pulling up the Ednalee newspaper, I scrolled through back issues—further and further back, years running past the computer screen like water in a river. The search bar was a handy feature, and when I typed in Carver, several entries popped up. Evidently, Judson had been involved in many litigations. As I read one account of a foreclosure, another Carver's name appeared: Charles Carver.

Absorbed in what I was reading, I felt as if I had been transported backward in time as I read about the tragedy of Charles Carver. Scanning further, I found Charles's name in several items. Evidently, Charles had an affliction—he was a gambling addict. Then, a bold-type headline caught my eye: *Heir to Carver fortune disappears.*

I lost track of time as I read what had been big news a number of years ago. Charles had run up debts. His debtors were after him and, if brought to trial, he faced a stiff penalty and jail time. Then, one day he simply disappeared.

Charles, it seemed, had mortgaged the Carver farm and, unable to repay it, had left town, leaving his brother Judson holding the bag.

The front page story ended. Hurriedly, I scanned the paper, finding another story I had overlooked, several days after the disappearance made the news. Judson had stepped forward and covered his brother's debts. The Carver estate was saved.

No one had been able to locate Charles and rumors were he might have traveled to South America. His wife declared her innocence and, unable to bear the shame, she and her young daughter moved, nobody knew where.

So, at last, here was a story of a benevolent side to Judson. He had paid off his brother's debts, leaving his sister-in-law free of that encumbrance. Evidently the two brothers had nothing in common when it came to finances. Everything Judson touched seemed to have prospered and nothing was said about further liens against the Carver estate.

I wished I could ask Miss Evangeline what she knew about this, but since that was impossible, I thought about Miss Ann. Would she remember that tragic episode in the life of the Carvers? Why hadn't she mentioned it to me when I talked to her earlier about Judson?

I left the library feeling far less elated than I had felt when I began my search. I had craved information and I found it. But, even though Charles's disappearance was long-ago news, I felt troubled about the heart-wrenching pain suffered by his family. It seemed a curse was hanging over the Carver estate.

Chapter 44

By the time I got home, I didn't feel like talking with anyone, not even Miss Ann, and the cold and windy day was dismal. My mind was busy with what I'd read at the library and the whole business of the deaths of three women associated with the Carver estate. So, because work is often an antidote to worry, or at least it keeps my hands busy as well as my mind, I grabbed a dust cloth and began polishing furniture.

I rubbed my lovely old piano until the wood gleamed. The piano had been left in one of the houses Daisy was selling. Instead of letting it go with the house and dealing with the possibility that the new owners might not want it, she gave it to me. Sitting down on the bench, I ran my hands over the keys, but all I could think of were sad songs of the 1950s. And I didn't need sad. The March wind, howling around the corner of the house, did nothing to lighten my mood.

I couldn't get the image of Charles Carver out of my mind. What had happened to him? Where had he gone when he disappeared? Did his wife and daughter join him? Where had he lived?

Assuredly, the wife would be dead by now, but surely the daughter was alive somewhere. Did I dare try to contact her or should I just let well enough alone?

It seemed that being connected in any way to the Carver family was dangerous. Could a curse actually hang over the estate? Did I believe in such things?

My dust cloth and I headed for the bookcase, and then, with it dust-free and shiny, I turned to the small table beside my front door. This table held the bonsai tree, the plant that had once belonged to Miss Evangeline and came to me by way of Jules. I picked up the bonsai to move it while I dusted, and it was at that moment Penny had one of her spells.

Now, Penny is usually a docile cat, easy to get along with, loves to nap, but occasionally, something, maybe just the joy of life or the dormant genes of her wild ancestors, emerges to overcome any inhibitions. She runs. No, not just runs—she tears out. She jumps and climbs, streaking through the house like her sanity has vanished. The vet says she's in perfect health and this is just her way of letting off steam.

And that's what she took in her mind to do today. Her erratic flight led her to the front room. Sounding like a herd of elephants, she leaped for the table, bumped into me, and knocked the bonsai tree from my hands.

The pot fell to the floor, breaking into two pieces and scattering plant and dirt across the boards. "Penny!" I yelled. "Stop that!"

Fearing what she would demolish next, I trotted to the family room. My cat lay on her rug in front of the fireplace, eyes closed, paws curling and uncurling, the picture of domesticity.

"Penny," I said, standing over her. "You're a naughty cat. Do you realize you've just broken a flowerpot and made a mess for me to clean up?"

She didn't open her eyes and ignored me.

Shaking my head, I returned to the front room. I would never understand the mind of a cat.

Such a shame that the bonsai plant had been an innocent victim. I bent to retrieve the small tree, which would need another container. Gingerly picking it up, I looked it over. It appeared unharmed except the roots were all knotted into a hard bunch. This was caused by years of neglect, probably, not by the fall to the floor.

The root system looked as if it hadn't been disturbed for quite some time. I didn't know much about bonsai, but I had heard that their roots should be trimmed periodically. The actual tree looked as if the top had been trimmed, but the tree didn't seem healthy. Perhaps Miss Evangeline didn't know how to properly care for it.

Gently, I shook away the excess dirt. I had thought the roots were just tangled in a knot, but that wasn't the case. They had grown around an object—a small, oblong box of some sort.

Carefully working the box loose without damaging the roots took several minutes, but at last a rusty metal container lay in my hand, separated from Miss Evangeline's plant.

How odd! I'd never heard of anything being buried beneath a plant—well, maybe things like that happened during the Civil War. I dimly recalled the story of an ancestor who had stuck her diamond ring into a pot of ferns when threatened by invading northern soldiers. So, if someone wanted to make sure it wasn't found, he might put it under a slow-growing bonsai.

My curiosity whetted, I took plant and box into the kitchen. I found a large bowl to temporarily house the bonsai. Carrying the bowl with me, I returned to the front room and scooped up enough of the loose dirt from the floor to pack around the roots and keep them from drying out. I put the bowl and plant on the table and hurried back to that fascinating box.

The lid of the box was rusted to the extent that it was hard to distinguish it from the rest of the box. Carrying the box with me, I traipsed to the utility room, rummaged in a drawer, and came up with a screwdriver. I ran this around the rim of the box, working it under the lid. By twisting the screwdriver, I was able to lever the lid upward. Rust flakes dropped into my hand as the lid came off and fell to the floor. I scooped up the lid and carried it and the box back to the dining room.

Placing the box on the table, I stirred the contents with one finger. A crumpled and torn plastic wrapping lay there. It came apart in my fingers as I picked it up. Within these scraps of plastic lay an old-fashioned pocket watch.

I gently lifted the watch from its tattered nest and held it under the ceiling light. The soft sheen of rose gold seemed to glow in my hand.

The glass over the face of the watch was broken and cloudy, but pinpoints of light glimmered from the golden rim. The largest diamond I had ever seen twinkled from the top of the watch face where the numeral twelve should have been.

This was an expensive piece of jewelry! What under the sun was it doing beneath a bonsai tree? And why did it have an ugly hole right through the center—a hole that went all the way through from front to back? The hole would have rendered it useless as a timepiece, but its apparent worth wouldn't have decreased much, because gold and jewels didn't lose their value with time.

Too stunned to move, I sat staring at it, trying to make sense of why anyone would have buried such an expensive item under dirt and left it there for years.

Carefully, I turned the watch over. The back of it, which also looked to be gold, was untarnished and bright. Carefully engraved there and partially obliterated by the hole were the initials CC.

How long did I sit, too stunned to move? Maybe it was because I had just come from the library where I had read about the disappearance of Charles Carver, or maybe it was because the plant had belonged to Miss Evangeline, but I immediately thought of the missing Carver heir. Had the watch belonged to him?

Shaking my head, I reached for my cell phone. "This is too much for me to deal with," I told Ulysses who lay under the table at my feet. "Cade can have this watch and decide what to do with it and what significance it has. I can't wait to be rid of it."

The truth was, for whatever reason the watch had been buried, the fact that somebody had seen fit to hide it away was ominous. It gave me an uneasy feeling. I wanted nothing to do with it.

Chapter 45

Cade held the watch lightly in the palm of his hand. He spoke to me without looking up. "You found this in a flowerpot and the pot once belonged to Miss Evangeline?" he asked.

I nodded. "Jules gave it to me before he left town. He was frightened, Cade, and he said he couldn't properly care for the tree anymore. He had no plans to return." I told Cade about my trip to the library and finding the newspaper accounts of Charles Carver's disappearance.

"Looks like it had been in that planter for a long time," Cade said. "The internal workings are ruined, but the gold case and those diamonds and rubies are worth as much as they ever were. More, maybe."

"But, why would such an expensive thing be hidden away under a plant? And those initials, Cade—could they stand for Charles Carver?"

He placed the watch on a piece of paper on his desk. "Well, since the bonsai tree was Miss Evangeline's and her uncle was Charles Carver, I'd say the answer to that is, 'probably.' But why? From what you've told me, the older Mr. Carver just disappeared, leaving his wife and daughter. She sold out and moved off—not sure where. Maybe Charles left the watch with his brother Judson for safekeeping. Or maybe it was to repay him for a loan."

"But, the hole, Cade. Why would Charles have put a hole in it? And, even with the hole, as you said, it's an expensive watch. Even though it's ruined for keeping time, keeping it in a bank vault would make more sense than sticking it into dirt for who knows how many years."

Cade was silent for so long, I thought he might not have heard me. He stood up and walked to the window, gazing out at the rain running in rivulets down the glass. Then, he turned to face me.

"Unless I miss my guess, that hole was made by a bullet," he said, "but who knows how many years ago the bullet was shot through the watch? And why? It could have been an accident, although I don't see how. Maybe it had been given to Mr. Carver as a gift and he was making sure no one saw that he had ruined it for keeping time."

A cold shiver ran down my back and I pulled my raincoat closer. "A bullet?" I whispered. "That was my thought too. It seems hardly likely that someone would shoot a watch accidentally."

"Another scenario, Ned," he went on. "If we're right about the initials being Charles Carver's, and if that hole is really a bullet hole, maybe Charles didn't just run off somewhere to escape his debt. If he was wearing this watch in his vest at the time that bullet went through, it's a pretty good bet that somebody killed him."

"But who, Cade? And if Judson saw the watch and knew someone had killed his brother, wouldn't he have moved heaven and earth to find the murderer?"

"Maybe, unless he knew who it was and was protecting them, or maybe he just didn't want further scandal. It was so long ago, Ned, and the people who might give us some answers are all dead."

I was silent, digesting this. Charles had disappeared decades ago. Everyone assumed he had gone somewhere, maybe changed his identity to escape his many debts. But, what if he hadn't? What if he had been killed and the killer disposed of the body? But then, how did Judson come by the watch? Surely Miss Evangeline hadn't shot her uncle and then took off his watch and hidden it in the dirt.

"Cade," I said, "I don't think Miss Evangeline knew what was under that bonsai tree. I think she kept it because it had been her father's. She would have been young when her uncle disappeared. Surely she wouldn't have shot him."

Cade shook his head. "I don't imagine there's anybody left who knows what happened. But, at some point in the past, somebody knew and kept it a secret for a good many years."

Chapter 46

Due to this month's changeable nature, the wind blew the clouds and rain away, and by the time darkness closed in, a round, silver moon shone down on Granger Mansion. I stood with a cup of chamomile tea in my hands, gazing out the window at the old well, the place I had caught my first glimpse of Ulysses. Only, at the time, I wasn't sure if he was a dog or a wolf howling at that mysterious moon, and I certainly had no idea that he would soon become my treasured housemate.

Sipping my tea, I thought about the things that had transpired since that night, the good and the bad. Maybe Pat was right—maybe bad things happened when the moon was full. If that were so, I should be extra cautious tonight because I had convinced Cade that I no longer needed his protective presence on my sofa. And this was the final full moon this month, a blue moon.

Shaking my head to dispel my nervousness at being alone, I took another sip of the chamomile tea. My fierce watchdog was in the house and I also firmly believed that the Lord was aware of all the things going on in His world. Besides, I couldn't continue to impose upon Cade's good-natured willingness to be my bodyguard.

"We'll be fine," I assured Ulysses who had padded over to admire the moon with me. "Not a thing to worry about. Whoever hit me on the head won't risk breaking in, and I certainly don't plan to make any more trips to the Carver house. Cade and Gerald and the sheriff are taking care of things, and the murderer, if he's smart, is keeping a low profile."

Reassured by my positive thoughts and fortified with the relaxing tea, I decided I'd go to bed. Hopefully, I'd sleep well and perhaps by tomorrow the mysteries surrounding those awful deaths would be solved. No longer would a murderer stalk the county.

Ulysses' low growl woke me. Groggily, I turned over and opened my eyes.

"What is it, Ulysses?" I whispered as I dropped my hand to his head. He stood stiff and alert on the floor beside my bed.

Moonlight flooded the room, making it seem almost like day. Whatever was happening outside was of interest to my dog. Maybe a raccoon or possibly a coyote?

Swinging my feet off the bed, I followed Ulysses to the window and peered out. Nothing moved in the yard below me. Even the trees were still—dark silhouettes against the moon.

"It's all right," I told my dog. "Probably you just heard an owl. You're a good boy, though, for being alert and on guard."

As I turned from the window, a movement caught my eye. One of the shadows in the yard below me moved. My breath caught in my throat. The dark shape of a person ran from behind a tree, a person crouching over and moving fast toward my front porch. A man? A woman? What was he doing in my yard at three o'clock in the morning?

Ulysses cut loose. He struck the window with his front feet, barking and growling, the hair on his back standing up.

The figure below us paused, then sprinted toward the street.

I ran for my phone and punched Cade's number. My heart was pounding so loudly, it nearly suffocated me. He answered, sounding half asleep, but he came awake instantly. "Stay away from the windows," he said. "Be sure your doors are locked. I'm on my way."

In my abject terror, I forgot about the gun in my table by the bed. I didn't think about it until I was halfway to the stairs, and I certainly wasn't going back for it.

I had heard that fear paralyzes a person. In slow motion, I moved out of the bedroom door, wanting to run, to fly down the stairs, dash to all the doors, and grab a weapon, but panic froze my muscles.

Ulysses stalked along with me, still muttering in his throat, as I checked the doors. I peeked out the dining room window and the front room window, but nothing moved. Everything was as still as if it were painted.

What was that figure doing out there? Would he double back, risking Ulysses' ire, and break out a window? Who was it? It seemed an eternity, but it was actually only a few minutes until Cade's truck roared up the drive and parked in front of the house. As he got out, Gerald jogged up the drive from the carriage house. Moonlight glint-ed off their two guns as they met, talked a minute, and disappeared around my house, one going one way, the other, the opposite way.

"Oh, Gerald, go back to Coradee," I whispered. "Don't leave her alone."

As if he heard me, Gerald reappeared and trotted back toward the carriage house.

Cade came inside and I ran to him, grabbing his hands. "Well?" I said. "Did you find anything?"

"Your car was unlocked," he said. "The glove compartment was opened. He took out some papers then just shoved most of them back inside. Probably he was nervous, in a hurry, and didn't care if you knew he'd been there."

It was hard to speak around the lump in my throat. "He was looking for something. Money? What?"

Cade shrugged. "Maybe money. Maybe something else. This is your second near-break-in. I'd say that somebody thinks you have some-thing that's important to him. Don't you lock your car at night?"

I nodded. "I usually do. I guess I forgot last night. It was a pretty unusual day and I just wasn't thinking about somebody trying to get into my car."

"Whoever it was vanished without leaving anything behind that we found," he said. "When daylight comes, I'll be able to search a little better. Surely he left something, a footprint, something. I think you should call Miss Ann and warn her about the prowler, to be sure she's safely locked in."

"Oh, I hope I don't scare her," I said. "But, she should be warned."

Miss Ann assured me she was fine and her burglar alarm was set. "No worries, Nettie," she said. "I'll stay up now and keep watch. I couldn't go back to sleep anyway. I'm glad Cade is with you."

Replacing the receiver, I turned to Cade. "Would you like some coffee?"

"Sounds good," he said. "I don't think either of us will get any more sleep."

As I filled the pot with water and measured coffee into the basket, I wondered aloud, "What would anyone want that I have, or what could they think I have? I'm no threat to anyone. I've backed off and am keeping away from the whole murderous bunch out at Carver farm."

"Maybe whoever was here tonight doesn't know you've backed off," Cade said, reaching into the cabinet for two cups. "And maybe it isn't someone from the Carver place. We don't know."

"The watch?" I asked. "Does someone know about the pocket watch?"

Cade shook his head. "I don't see how anyone could. It evidently had been buried a long time. If anybody at the farm knew it was there, it would've been dug up a long time ago."

We sat together on the sofa in front of the fireplace, an afghan across our legs. No fire burned in the fireplace, but I didn't need it to feel warm and safe. Cade's arm was around me. We talked and drank coffee until the sun rose. The terror of the night subsided, and despite night prowlers and threats from an unknown source, I was content.

Chapter 47

I'd barely had my first cup of coffee the next morning when Daisy called. "Ned," she said, "can you come to my office? The owner of that property you're interested in is here with me. If you still want to buy it, I believe she's ready to sell."

I felt my heart quicken. "I sure am interested. I'll be there as soon as I can get into some jeans. We had a bit of excitement around here last night and after Cade left, I'm afraid I dozed off for a bit."

Cade had been gone when I awoke, but if he had found any evidence of last night's prowler, he surely would have told me. So, that was another unsolved mystery. The good news from Daisy did a lot to help chase away the night's terror. I could hardly wait to hear what I'd need to do to be able to buy that large lot that had sheltered my parents and me. I needed this bright spot in the day.

By noon I was the proud owner of my old homestead. It was a good feeling. To celebrate, I called Pat and Jackie and asked them to meet me at Grandy's, coffee on me. I also called Cade. He offered his congratulations and said he was glad it was back in the Duncan family's hands.

Janey smiled as I walked through Grandy's door. A strong March wind had blown away the clouds, but it was a cold wind, a winter wind. Even the timid, pale green leaves on the trees looked as if they wished they hadn't been so eager to make their appearance.

"There'll be two more coming, Janey," I said, heading to my favorite booth at the back. "I'll want mocha coffee, but I'm not sure what Pat and Jackie will have."

I was warming my hands around my mug when my two best friends slid into the bench across from me.

"When are you going to take us out to see your property?" Pat asked as Janey came to take their order.

"Any time you'd like," I answered. "I'm so excited, I can't see straight."

"What do you plan to do with it?" Jackie asked.

"Oh, goodness, I don't know. Maybe I've been foolish, but I just couldn't stand to see it neglected. I might build another house or just keep it mowed. It'd be pretty as a park. I could put in some flowers and benches and maybe a fish pond and—"

"I'm glad you decided to buy," Jackie interrupted. "You aren't planning to move out of your old house, are you?"

I shook my head. "Not at all. I love that old place."

Pat grinned. "I like the way you do things—for no reason except that you want to."

Cade slid in beside me, bringing a cold breath of air with him. He smelled outdoorsy with a touch of leather and his spicy aftershave, a good, comforting scent. He covered my hand with his cold one and smiled at me, his eyes dancing.

"You'll have to take me out to your new property," he said. "When we both have time, that is. Today, I'm kind of snowed under, but I'm glad you bought it, Ned. Land is always a good investment."

I nodded. "How about a cup of coffee?"

He shook his head. "Not today. Nothing new about last night's prowler. Maybe he'll decide you don't have whatever it is he wants and let you alone."

"I wish I could put an ad in the paper or signs all over town saying, *Notice to all crooks. Look elsewhere. I have nothing of value to you.*"

Pat lifted her coffee cup as if she were going to offer a toast. "Good idea. Or, I could tell my ladies' circle in church. Those women are better than a newspaper for spreading stories."

178

Cade fidgeted and cleared his throat. He spoke to all of us, but he was gazing at me, his eyes shining. "While you are all three together, I need to tell you my big news, and it's all right with me if you tell everybody you know." He paused and took a breath. "My little girl, you remember her, Jackie? Pat? Marianne is coming home."

Marianne? His little girl? No wonder he was excited.

"That's great!" Pat said. "I haven't seen her since she left for the mission field."

Jackie reached across the table and squeezed his arm. "Me either. No wonder you're beaming."

I couldn't think of anything to say. My friends knew Marianne, had probably watched her grow up. They had known Lena, Cade's wife, too. But I had never seen either Marianne or Lena. All I knew of them was what I had heard. Lena had died last year and now lay in one of those lonely graves at the cemetery where Uncle Javin and Miss Evangeline were buried. All I knew about Marianne was that she was a missionary to a remote tribe in Africa. But this was Cade's child and he was overjoyed that she was coming home. I would be too, if she were mine, and I was glad for Cade's sake.

Smiling at Cade, who was looking at me anxiously, I said, "That's certainly big news. Tell us more. Will she be here soon?"

He nodded. "She's flying into the Tulsa airport. I'll go tonight and pick her up. She said she's bringing a surprise, but she wouldn't say what. I just know she's coming home, and it has been too long since she's been here."

It seemed to me that Marianne's appearance was surprise enough without bringing anything extra. Why hadn't she told her father more?

"It'll be wonderful to finally meet her, Cade," I said, and I meant it. "I know she's a wonderful person. I'm glad she's coming, and I can hardly wait for her to get here."

A snatch of "Ghost Riders" interrupted, and Cade glanced at his phone.

"Looks like I've got to go. We're closing in on that teen gang that's been causing trouble. You three have fun." He grinned at us and scooted from the booth.

I gazed at Cade's retreating figure until he went out the door. My friends were staring at me.

"You look like you're in shock," Jackie said.

Taking a deep breath, I said, "Maybe I am. That was certainly a bolt from the blue."

Pat drained the last of her coffee. "There's no reason to think Marianne'll change your relationship with Cade. You'll love her. Best I remember, she's a sweet girl."

"I'm sure she is. I'm happy for him."

Marianne's sweetness or lack of it didn't concern me. How it would influence Cade's and my relationship did concern me. A daughter would be sharing Cade's life, and rightly so. I wasn't proud of the fact that I was wary of sharing Cade. To be honest, I didn't know whether I was glad or sorry.

Chapter 48

The house phone was ringing as I walked in the front door. Hurrying to answer, I checked caller ID and didn't recognize the number. Was it a crank call? The same mysterious voice that had called with a warning? I could let the machine answer, or I could pick it up and try to put an end to this. If this was the same man who had called before, warning me to back off from the Carver murders, now was my chance to tell him I was out of it, well and good, and he could stop pestering me.

"Hello?" I said, speaking into the receiver.

A deep male voice came across the line. "Look, I'm tired of playing games, Miz McNeil. You have something we want. Miss Evangeline was seen handing it to you, the night before she died. Bring it with you to the farm and do it quick. You have thirty minutes and that's all. Better get started if you want to see your precious dog alive again."

My heart lurched and my breath caught in my throat. My dog? Frantically, I searched the room, calling Ulysses. No answering bark greeted me. I didn't hear him anywhere. I ran upstairs, looking into every room, then down again. Carrying the phone with me, I rushed from window to window, straining to catch a glimpse of Ulysses anywhere in the yard. Both house and yard were empty.

Anger boiled like a geyser inside me, choking me—anger and fear.

I licked my dry lips. My lungs felt squeezed as I choked out the words. "Do you have my dog? Why? What have you done with him?

You'd better not hurt him in any way, do you hear me? It'll be the last vile thing you do if you harm Ulysses."

He laughed, a low and sinister sound. "I don't believe you have anything to say about it. If you value that hound, you'd better bring what Miss Evangeline gave you and come to the main house at the farm. Now. Don't tell your boyfriend cop or those two you hang around with. Remember, your dog is at our mercy. Come alone. If there's any sign that you've brought company, you'll never see your pet again. I'd advise you to hurry."

I heard Ulysses bark and then the line went dead.

My hands shook as I replaced the receiver. Taking a deep breath, I tried to think clearly. The Carver kin believed Miss Evangeline had given me something. What? The watch? Her last wishes? Her will? Then it hit me. They weren't sure what she had given me. They hadn't named anything. What did they think she gave me? A will? Whose will, hers or Judson Carver's? Or did they think she had given me something that would incriminate one of them?

My whirling brain settled on one thought: if they believed she had given me a will, I'd be happy to produce one. Trotting to my desk, I pulled out a white, legal-size envelope. Folding a couple of pieces of white paper, I slid them inside. On the outside of the envelope, I scribbled, Last Will and Testament. Then, I stuffed it into my purse.

All I could think about was Ulysses at the mercy of those ruthless people. If someone out there hadn't blinked at murdering three women, what chance did he have?

Even in my agitation, I knew I'd better let someone know what was happening, but if I told anyone, it might put Ulysses in danger. Cade would be in Tulsa with Marianne. He might not even come over tonight, or maybe he would and he'd bring Marianne with him. I should be back with Ulysses in hand long before anyone knew I was gone, but just in case I wasn't, I scribbled a note saying Ulysses had been kidnapped and I had gone to the farm. Leaving it under a coffee cup on the dining table, I slipped into my coat and ran out to my car.

Thoughts whirled through my mind as I drove like a madwoman over the roads toward the Carver farm. I would wave the envelope under the kidnapper's nose and hope he believed it was a will, but as soon as he saw what was inside, Ulysses and I would be in jeopardy. What could I do to stall until we were in my car and on our way back home? I would have to play it by ear, and I prayed that I could bluff them. I didn't have a plan beyond doing whatever it took to get Ulysses safely away.

The countryside passed in a blur as I sped toward the Carver mansion. At last, the turnoff to the house came in sight. I yanked the steering wheel. The car slid, then righted itself. Braking at the end of the drive, I leaned my head on the wheel, breathed a prayer, and tried to think of what I should do next. Take the envelope with me? Tell them I had it but they wouldn't get it until Ulysses was safe with me? I pushed my purse under the front seat and slammed out of the car. If they couldn't see the envelope, at least they couldn't take it away from me. Maybe I'd have a few minutes to get Ulysses into the car.

The mansion loomed before me, imposing and grim. Why had I ever thought it was beautiful? It was a large, forbidding pile of bricks that housed people who would stop at nothing to achieve their aim.

I started up the walk, then paused as a portion of sanity returned. If I entered the house, I would be at the mercy of those who waited there. So would Ulysses. Not a good move. I would make them come to me.

Anger settled down from being hot and consuming into a cold, deadly knot in my stomach. I refused to be a victim. This person—or persons, as the case might be—was evil. I would not let them get the upper hand. I would not go to them, obedient and frightened. Returning to my car, I leaned inside and pressed the horn. I kept pressing it, filling the deadly quiet with sound.

The voice behind me was loud. "Quit that infernal noise."

I jumped and whirled around. No one was there. The person had spoken from the shelter of the trees.

"Give me that paper," it said.

I took a deep breath to steady my voice. "You've got to be crazy. Give me my dog first."

"The paper," he said.

I put my hand on the car's door handle. "No."

A low laugh sent chills down my spine. From the shadows of the trees stepped a tall, dark figure. Mick Morrow. As he came toward me, I contemplated trying to jump back into my car, but I knew I wouldn't be able to scramble inside and lock the door before he reached me. I felt for my cell phone and remembered I had dropped it into my purse after recharging it the night before, and my purse was under the seat.

I edged around the front of the car, closer and closer to the house. If I ran, so would Morrow, and his legs were longer than mine. I backed up, keeping my eyes on Mick. He came toward me, taking his time and grinning as I walked backward. I didn't know I had reached the house until I stumbled on the steps. Fumbling behind me, I felt the door and turned the knob. The door swung open.

Like a shot, a blur of fur and fury rushed past me and launched himself at Mick. Ulysses! He was alive.

Morrow stumbled and went down under my dog's onslaught. His head whacked the sidewalk and he lay still.

Tears of relief moistened my eyes. "Good boy, Ulysses," I said as he looked up at me. He started toward me, tail wagging, a goofy grin on his face, but before he could reach me, hands grabbed my arms, yanked me inside the building, and slammed the door.

184

Chapter 49

I heard Ulysses hit the door and heard him whine. "Go home, Ulysses!" I yelled. "Get help. Home, boy."

Did he hear me? Did he understand? The person who had grabbed me yanked my arms up behind my shoulder blades and pain shot through me.

"Forget your dog," a female voice said. "We'll let you go as soon as you hand it over."

"It's in my purse," I gasped.

I felt ropes go around my wrists. "Get a blindfold on her," the unseen woman said. "No need for her to see any more than she's already seen. Somebody may be out looking for her, and we don't want her found. Take her upstairs."

"What are we going to do with her?" This voice was feminine too and sounded scared. Pearly?

Someone gave me a push. "I don't know. We'll think about it. Too many deaths already. We've got to make sure that the estate is in our hands before those cops figure out too much."

I stumbled along in front of them.

The second person spoke again. "Where is your purse, Ned?"

The first woman, who, I was pretty sure, was Veda, gave my arms a vicious tug. I bit my lip to keep from yelling. What should I say? I'd left it in my SUV, but I wasn't going to tell these two. Why make it easier?

Figuring that a lie was forgivable when it meant a difference between life and death, I said, "Your pal Mick Morrow got it. When Ulysses hit him, I saw the purse fly out of his hands."

"Go get it," Veda ordered Pearly.

"You go get it," Pearly said. "That dog of hers is out there, standing over Mick."

Veda muttered something under her breath. "Well, go get your gun. Shoot it. Do I have to tell you everything?"

Anger dissolved the last remnants of fear. I kicked backward as hard as I could and felt my boot connect with a shin.

"Ow!" I assumed it was Veda's leg my boot had made contact with, and I assumed she wasn't injured so much that she couldn't shove me, because she did. I fell forward into what was probably the newel post.

Veda moaned and groaned. "You take her upstairs," she said to Pearly. "Here. Take this gun. I'll get the other one. Soon as I can walk."

"Be sure you don't shoot Mick," Pearly said.

Veda's voice was harsh. "Why should you care? With him out of the way, that'd take care of another problem."

My arms ached, my head ached, and I was sick with fear for Ulysses' safety. Pearly gave me a push. I stumbled onto the stairs and started up them.

"We've got another flight," she said as we reached the first landing. "You know, I'm really sorry about all this. I wish you hadn't gotten involved. I like you, but you insisted, didn't you? Has anyone ever told you you're too nosy for your own good?"

I sighed. "Seems I've heard that before."

I was breathless by the time we climbed the second set of stairs. And cold. This upper part of the house didn't feel like it was heated. I heard a door open. Pearly prodded me with what must have been a gun barrel and propelled me inside a room. She closed the door behind me. I heard her footsteps going downstairs.

Fighting a rising feeling of panic, I tried to slow my racing thoughts and heart. I couldn't see, my arms were tied behind me, and I had no

186

way of knowing what was happening to Ulysses. What should I do now? How was I going to get my dog and myself out of this mess? They wouldn't find my purse with Mick or anywhere else except in my car. When would they think to start searching it? And then what would happen?

Chapter 50

I remembered looking up at this third floor from outside the house and seeing windows. Presumably, at least one of those windows was in this room, but how would I find it? Should I bump around the walls with my head until I touched glass? Should I turn around and try to feel it with my hands that were tied behind my back? I'd try the head method first, but before that, I'd need to find the wall.

Locating a wall wasn't hard. I slid around until a solid object stopped me. Was the room furnished? Had I found an old wardrobe closet or was this indeed one side of a room? Turning my back to it, I felt along it as I slid sideways. Good! It seemed to be a wall. Facing it, I bumped along with my head again, hoping to feel a cold, hard pane of glass. My head ached already, and this method was hard work. I turned with my back to the wall once more, feeling for a different surface as I slid sideways across the floor, crab-like.

At last, my fingers touched the cold surface of a pane of glass. The sill should be just below it. Bending low, I probed the wood until I felt the horizontal sill. Could I use the edge of it to slide off my blindfold? I knelt on the floor, leaned my head against the sill, and rubbed my blindfold across it. Up, down. Veda had done an excellent job of making that binding hard to dislodge. My nose and my forehead were raw and scraped but I felt the cloth slip a little. I licked my dry lips and rubbed again. The blindfold slid a little more. Hooking the edge of it under a corner of the sill, I lifted my head. The cloth slipped down around my neck and I could see.

Never had the gray light of late afternoon looked so good. My prison appeared to be a small, empty room complete with cobwebs and dust. Nothing was in it except an old wood bed frame with a faded and torn spread across it and a faded oriental rug under it. I turned to glance out of the window. The figures of Veda and Pearly were small down below me on the sidewalk. My heart sank as I saw Mick move. He hadn't been out nearly long enough. Doubtless, he would now join in the search for my purse. But, there was no sign of Ulysses anywhere and I hadn't heard a shot. My heart lifted. He must be safe. Hopefully, he was no longer on the estate but was heading back home.

If I broke the window, could I use it to cut the rope that bound my hands? Would the people on the ground hear it break? I would have to risk it, but what could I use? Nothing in the room was movable. There were no vases, no lamps, nothing that might crack a window. I glanced at the floor. I had my boots.

I was not contortionist enough to use my hands to remove a boot, so I'd try to push it off with my other foot. I pushed against the heel of the boot and wriggled my toes, glancing out the window now and then at the figures below. They had moved to my car. It wouldn't take them long to find my purse and the empty envelope.

Perspiration was running down my face by the time I had my boot off. I lay down on my back, grabbed my boot, and backed up to the window. I didn't have much leverage, but I swung it at the window. Nothing happened. I tried again and heard the glass crack. The third whack broke the glass and cool air rushed in.

I backed against the glass until I felt a jagged piece prick my wrist. It hurt, but it was my only hope. Carefully, I sawed the ropes over the broken edge. A warm trickle of blood oozed down my hand, but at last, the rope gave. One more movement and the fibers parted. My hands were free.

With the rope dangling from my wrist, I glanced out the window again. The three of them had left my car and were moving toward the house. They would soon reach the door and be up the stairs. When they came into this room, what would they do? Add me to their long list of casualties?

My heart pounded as my gaze swept the room. No closet, no bathroom, no other door except the one through which Pearly had shoved me. Probably, the other rooms on this floor were as bare as this one with no place to hide. I heard the front door slam. It was too late to run downstairs and try to make it out the back way. The bed was my only hope. Could I slide under it? Would the tattered spread be long enough to hide me? That would probably be the first place those three would look, but it seemed to be my only chance unless I climbed through the broken window, but if I jumped, the fall would probably kill me.

No sensible way of escape came to me in a blinding flash of wisdom. In fact, wisdom and good sense had pretty much flown under a severe attack of panic. Would trickery work? If I could make them think I had crawled out the window, I might gain a few more minutes. Picking up my boot, I used it to clear a larger space of broken glass. Then I tugged off the blindfold which hung around my neck and laid it across the sill. I could see that the roof jutted out a few feet above a narrow brick ledge. Could I climb out, hang onto the eave, and, hugging the outer wall, inch away from the window so they couldn't see me? I took a good look at the ground far below, the narrowness of the ledge, and the lack of a good place on the roof to hang onto. I was never all that athletic, and what agility I'd once had disappeared with age. Besides, even for Tarzan, it'd be quite a feat. But, if I could make my enemies think I'd managed to do that . . .

A few drops of blood from my wrist spattered the floor. I shook free of the rope, rubbed it around in the blood, and carefully draped it across the sill.

Footsteps and voices echoed down the hall, heading toward my prison room, as I tugged off my other boot and ran toward the bed. Waiting until I heard their voices nearing the door, I breathed a prayer, took aim, and threw my boot through the window, shattering the remaining glass with a loud crash. My heart pounding, I rolled under the bed just as the door burst open.

Chapter 51

Veda yelled. "What? Where is she?"

"The window," Pearly said. "The idiot woman went out the window. She broke the glass and jumped."

Footsteps ran from the door to the window. "If she did," Mick said, "she's not going to be a problem. Nobody could have made that jump. She's not on the ledge. She's somewhere down below. Maybe she landed in the shrubbery."

"If she's not dead now, she'll wish she were," Veda said. "What a dirty trick she played, and I won't let her get away with it."

I bit my lip. Talk about the pot calling the kettle black!

"Where's Elbert, anyway?" Mick said. "He's never around when he's needed."

"He's out with the surveyors," Pearly answered.

"First, we've got to make sure that woman is out of commission. We'll find her, and whether she's dead or alive, we'll hide her good so her policeman boyfriend won't find her," Veda said. "And we've got to move her car, put it in the barn and cover it with hay. We can't have any trace of her around here at all. Well, get a move on!"

They clattered from the room. Their footsteps grew fainter on the stairs. I rolled out from under the bed and pushed myself up. I was alive for the time being, but for how long?

Now was my chance to slip down the stairs and out the back door. I'd never seen a back door in this house, but there had to be one.

Maybe it was in the pantry. Wherever it was, I'd find it. I'd have to. These people were killers. They were going to make sure Cade and whoever else came looking would find no trace that I had been here. But, when would Cade get here? Was he still in Tulsa? How about Ulysses? Was he on his way back to Ednalee?

I ran into the hall and down the first flight of stairs. So far, so good. Hopefully, they were still trying to find where I'd landed when I jumped. But, it wouldn't take long until they realized they'd been fooled, and then they would tear the place apart trying to find me.

I didn't pause when I reached the second floor. I ran down those stairs and into the kitchen. Then, I heard the back door open, somewhere beyond the pantry. I was trapped.

The fireplace had been my hiding place once before. Mick hadn't found me there. Maybe it would work again. It had better. There was nowhere else to go.

I edged into the inglenook behind the chair in front of the fireplace. It wasn't a very deep hiding place, but it was dark. Squatting down, I made myself as small as I could and held my breath. My breathing came in bursts, my heart pounding so loudly that surely someone would hear it. I prayed fervently that nobody would.

Elbert walked in through the pantry just as the other three rushed in from outside.

"What's going on?" Elbert asked. "Where's Mrs. McNeil? Did she bring it?"

"We don't know where she is!" Veda shouted. "She didn't bring anything—it was a trick."

She was a fine one to talk about a trick, but Elbert seemed clueless.

"So, where is she now?" Elbert asked. "Is she here?"

Pearly grabbed her husband's arm. "While you were mapping out a site for the casino, she came, got away from us, and hid. She's got to be here somewhere. Did you see anyone around the outbuildings?"

"I would have seen her if she was out there, and she's not. So, what do we do now?"

"Be prepared for the cops to show up," Mick said. "We can hide all traces of her and see if we can make her boyfriend believe us, or we can get out of here. I'm for getting out. I don't think you're ever going to get that money, and Pearly, you'd better come up with what you owe the casino or your hide won't hold shucks."

Pearly whimpered. "I told you I'd get it. Just be a little patient."

Mick snorted.

Veda got up in Mick's face. "Listen to me. We've come this far. You're not getting out of it now. You're just as guilty as I am. Myra got cold feet. Lila was dangerous. You know what happened to them?"

Mick's voice was deadly cold. "Are you threatening me?"

Elbert broke in. "This was all your idea, Veda, and I think you're as crazy as a loon. Crazy! Do you hear me? You're the one who killed Evangeline. Myra too. And Lila. All for your revenge and to get the estate. We're innocent."

Veda shoved over a kitchen chair. With one violent movement, she swept the flower arrangement off the dining table. "You were all willing to help and keep quiet until things got a little rough!" she shouted. "If I go to jail, you're going too." Veda's voice rose a few decibels until she was shrieking. "You know this whole estate should be mine. You know Evangeline had it only because her father was a murderer. Cowards! All of you!"

Good! They were turning against each other. But, what did Veda mean about the estate being hers? This sounded like the ravings of a lunatic.

Pearly, Elbert, and Mick started for the stairs. Veda ran after them, yelling that they couldn't leave.

I bit my lip. Now was my chance. While they were out of the room, I'd run out the back door. I could hide in the woods. I could . . . well, I'd think about it after I got out of this house.

My legs felt cramped from hunkering down and being wedged into a small space. Bracing my hands against the wall of the inglenook, I pushed myself to my feet. With no warning, the bricks under my hand gave way, and my arm plunged into a cavity in the wall. I touched something—something hard and cold. In the dim light, I saw a white thing—white and hideous. When my fingers brushed it, it fell. I gasped, horrified. I was looking down at the skull of a skeleton.

Before I could stop it, the shock that froze me in place rose from my throat, and I screamed. The clatter of falling bricks would surely bring that murderous crew to the kitchen, and if they hadn't heard that noise, they would have heard my scream. Anyone within two miles could have heard it. I didn't have time to ponder what I'd uncovered. I didn't have time to think. My instinct to survive took over, and I ran.

Chapter 52

The back door was indeed in the pantry. I dashed through and was in the yard. Behind me, I heard the yells and curses of the deranged people who were bent on killing me. No time to plan where to go. The woods were too far away but before me yawned the opening to the maze. I hesitated only for a moment. When there's no place else to hide, one takes the only thing available. I didn't stop to think. I just hurtled into that dreaded place.

At times, extreme terror sharpens the wits. At this moment, I feared the mob behind me more than I feared the tunnel. From a few decades ago came the voice of my friend Jackie. *Just put your hand on the right side of the maze,* she had said, *and take every right turn. You'll find your way out.* So, that is what I did.

I didn't slow down as I slid my hand along that bushy wall, following each right turn of the boxwood. The Carvers rushed in behind me. I heard their shouts and threats. Did they know the secret of escape too?

I was gasping for air and my side felt like it was going to break, but I kept running. Was Jackie right? Would this right hand solution really work? As if in sympathy with my predicament, rain began falling as dusk moved in.

The voices of my pursuers still followed but they were no longer together. Some of their words came from one direction, some from another. They were lost! With that encouraging realization, I burst from the maze into wonderful, wet, cloudy freedom. My legs would no longer hold me up. I collapsed onto the ground and gulped air, like a fish out of water.

Desperation gave me strength. The will to survive is a wonderful thing. Struggling to my feet, I trotted as fast as my bare feet allowed down the driveway. Maybe I could reach the main road before they found their way out. I could still hear them, back in that convoluted maze. Any minute, they would be after me again. The only sensible thing then would be to head for the trees that surrounded the driveway. But, until they escaped the confines of that bushy prison, I could make better time on the road.

I heard a car approaching. Who else? Reinforcements? I dodged behind a large oak and waited. Cade's truck roared into sight, tires slinging water as he gunned the engine.

Relief welled up within me and, with no warning, my strength left me as weak as a limp dishrag. I stumbled into the road, waving my arms.

Cade and Gerald jumped from the truck and ran to me. Cade held me tight.

"Cade," I panted, "they're all there—lost in the maze. The Carvers and Mick, they're trying to kill me."

"Get in the truck," he said.

Gerald helped me into the cab before climbing in beside me. A furry head and a wet, sloppy tongue greeted me. Ulysses! He too was in the front seat and, with a whimper of welcome, climbed onto my lap and began washing my face with his slobbery tongue. I grabbed him and held on.

Tires spun as Cade floored the accelerator. At the end of the driveway, he braked. He and Gerald jumped out and jogged toward the maze, guns drawn. Elbert and Pearly burst from the exit, panting and wheezing. Behind them came Mick and Veda. Their faces registered shock then resignation as they faced two guns leveled at them. Without a word, all four of them raised their hands. It was over.

Chapter 53

Pat shook her head. "This is unbelievable. Veda is guilty of murdering those three women because she hated Miss Evangeline and felt the estate should be hers?"

Cade sat on my sofa, a cup of coffee balanced on his knee. I was on one side of him, Marianne on the other. "That's about the size of it," he said. "You see, Veda was Charles Carver's daughter, the little girl who disappeared with her mother after his death. She blamed Judson for murdering her father, and I imagine she was right in that—at least, circumstantial evidence points to that."

"Do you mean the walled-up skeleton?" Ken asked.

Cade nodded. "That and the watch with Charles's initials on it. Looks like Judson may have shot Charles and sealed him up in the fireplace. That hole through the expensive watch was made by a long-ago bullet. Theorizing what happened, because nobody now can prove it, I'd say Judson didn't want to see his brother lose the estate and shot him, making it look like Charles had run out on his debts and his family. And Judson had a love of money that wouldn't allow him to get rid of the watch. He couldn't sell it either without fear of incriminating himself, so he buried it and kept it in the house."

Pat shuddered. "What an evil old man. His own brother!"

Jackie took a sip of her coffee and shook her head. "Ned, I can't imagine the shock of finding that skeleton sealed up in the fireplace. I'd have fainted dead away."

I put my coffee cup on the floor and gazed into the flames of the fireplace. Although it was April, the day was cold and drizzly, but the chill I felt had nothing to do with the weather. "I didn't have time to faint," I said. "If you'd been in my place, you'd have done what I did— run."

"I'm just glad nobody was hurt when you apprehended them," Marianne said, gazing at Cade with eyes that were so much like his. "It sounds awfully Old West to me."

Ken smiled at her. I'd noticed she had captured much of his interest throughout the evening.

Coradee sighed. "Uncle Moe is still on the loose, somewhere. I wish he'd give himself up. He's bound to be cold and hungry. I'll be glad when Gerald gets his law degree. Surely being a lawyer is safer than being a lawman."

Ron shook his head. "I wouldn't count on that. Lawyers know a lot of secrets, and since they do, sometimes folk figure they know too much for their own good."

"Real estate people too," Daisy said. "I need more coffee. Anyone else?" She left her seat by the fireplace and went to the kitchen.

"So, Pearly and Elbert helped that poor Veda woman because they were so greedy and wanted to inherit Eva's estate?" Miss Ann asked. "Greed can certainly destroy lives." She shook her head.

"That and because Pearly was desperate for money to pay her gambling debts," Gerald said. "She and Elbert were basically destitute due to her habit."

"I can see why Lila was murdered, if she actually knew that Veda killed Miss Evangeline," Jackie said. "But, why Myra?"

Cade answered. "Veda wouldn't talk, but Pearly had no problem telling everything she knew. According to her, the plan to kill Miss Evangeline was entirely Veda's. She convinced Myra that Miss Evangeline deserved to die because of the harm Judson had done to Myra's family. Myra's part in the murder was to hide behind a bush, wave a tablecloth from the kitchen, and scare Miss Evangeline's mare. She did that and then saw Veda rush out of hiding and hit Miss Evangeline with a hammer—your hammer, Ken. I think Veda wore gloves so the only prints on it were yours."

Ken shook his head. "And to think, I actually liked Myra."

Gerald took up the story. "Myra got cold feet—her conscience started bothering her, according to Pearly. She was going to tell what she knew, so Veda killed her too. Pearly and Elbert were afraid of Veda, and they knew they were in too deep to back out."

Marianne shook her head. "She must have been as certifiably crazy as anyone ever was."

"I wish Greta could have been here tonight," I said as I helped Daisy refill cups and pass a plate of Miss Ann's shortbread. "She's trying to track down Jules to tell him it's safe to come home."

"Why go to all the trouble of getting you out to the farm?" Miss Ann asked. "And was that a Carver who went through your car and tried to break into your house? What did they think you had?"

"Myra had seen Miss Evangeline hand me something," I said. "They were afraid it was a will and she had left them out. Miss Eva had confided in Lila about Ken being her son. Lila let it slip when she knew that the others were counting on inheriting. They were afraid she'd leave everything to him. They had to stop Miss Evangeline before she saw Ron and made out a will. They knew she didn't trust them and thought she had given me some sort of written statement of her intentions or suspicions."

I blinked away tears. "Poor lady. I think she was trying to undo some of her father's meanness. Ken, I'm glad you were in protective custody because you would surely have been next."

Ken grinned. "After you, cousin."

The two children on the floor smiled up at me and took their third helpings of shortbread. Mike, Ron and Jackie's new son with his shock of blond hair that was always falling into his eyes, and Bonnie, with her curly brown hair and large brown eyes, seemed comfortable and at home in the company of so many adults. Bonnie was the surprise Marianne had brought home with her. Bonnie's parents, also missionaries, had died in a small plane crash and, since Marianne was her godmother and Bonnie had no close relatives, Bonnie's care and well-being were entrusted to her.

Bonnie sat on the floor with Penny on her lap while Mike stroked Ulysses' silky ears. It was nice, the way children added a hominess to this old house of mine. I would talk to Cade and Marianne about her plans. Cade's small house must be crowded with two extra people, and mine was empty except for Ulysses, Penny, and me. My thoughts were interrupted by Jackie.

"Did anybody ever find that trust Judson Carver made out?" she asked.

"No, not yet," Cade answered. "What about it, Ron? Do Miss Evangeline's wishes hold up as a will?"

Ron cleared his throat. "That birth certificate of Ken's pretty much declares that he's the heir to the Carver estate, so nothing has really been decided yet. I'm conferring with a team of lawyers in the city. Looks to me like the farm belongs to Ken."

Ken shook his head. "I don't want it."

A chorus of surprised voices greeted that statement.

"Too much bad stuff has happened because of that farm," Ken said. "Oh, I'd like to take possession of the horses, maybe, just to be sure they have a nice home, but I wouldn't feel right about it. You know, there's a law about not profiting from a murder and, I'm sad to say, it looks like my grandfather may have murdered my great-uncle."

"Don't be too hasty about such a huge decision," I said. "You can't help what your ancestors did, and besides, nobody can prove that's what happened."

"This has been a really awful time," Ken said, "but I feel blessed anyway. I've discovered a new cousin, and I've found out who I am by birth. Besides, I like Ednalee. I'm thinking I just may settle down here." Marianne returned his smile.

Pat finished her coffee and set her cup on the floor. "Marianne, don't get the wrong idea about our little town. It's usually peaceful and filled with lovely people. The fault for all this lies with the moon. There was a blue moon in March, you know. It affects people who have a natural evil tendency. I believe the Carver family and Mick too were actually moonstruck."

I shook my head at my superstitious friend. A log dropped in the fireplace, sending a shower of sparks up the chimney. I sat down again beside Cade, gazed around the room at my circle of friends, and listened to the quiet chatter of the children on the floor. Cade slipped his arm around me and I leaned against his shoulder.

"I think you're wise, Ken," I said. "Friendship and family are worth much more than money could ever buy."

~ *The End* ~

But wait . . . there's more!

Don't miss the rest of
THE NED MCNEIL MYSTERY SERIES
Cozy mysteries with an extra shiver!!

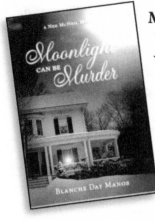

MOONLIGHT CAN BE MURDER

When widow Nettie "Ned" McNeil returns to her hometown of Ednalee, Oklahoma, she finds her uncle lying in a pool of blood. Obsessed, she risks her own life pursuing the killer who will stop at nothing to hide a deadly secret.

**Read a FREE chapter
or get your copy today at

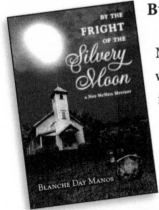

BY THE FRIGHT OF THE SILVERY MOON

Ned McNeil is haunted by a nightmare that wakes her in the middle of the night, leaving her gasping for breath. A dog—or is it a wolf?—howling in her yard under the brilliant autumn moon sends chills down her spine. Get ready for a page turner; a cozy mystery with an extra shiver that just may keep you up at night, even when the moon isn't full!

**Read a FREE chapter or get your copy today at

And don't miss the first four
DARCY AND FLORA MYSTERIES!
Also from the pen of Blanche Day Manos

The Cemetery Club ~ **Darcy & Flora Cozy Mystery #1**
Get your FREE chapter at www.Pen-L.com/TheCemeteryClub.html

Grave Shift ~ **Darcy & Flora Cozy Mystery #2**
Get your FREE chapter at www.Pen-L.com/GraveShift.html

Best Left Buried ~ **Darcy & Flora Cozy Mystery #3**
Get your FREE chapter at www.Pen-L.com/BestLeftBuried.html

Grave Heritage ~ **Darcy & Flora Cozy Mystery #4**
at www.Pen-L.com/GraveHeritage.html

Get your copy or a free chapter now!

Acknowledgments

A big thank you to my publisher, editors, cover designer, and to my wonderful Cozy Critter critique group and first readers. Also, thanks to each member of my family, including my brothers Tracy and Richard, and all the many who encouraged me, never losing faith in Ned McNeil and her ability to solve mysteries.

About the Author

In her previous life, Blanche Day Manos was a kindergarten teacher, part-time writer of feature stories for a newspaper, and writer of stories and poems for children's and Christian magazines. Now, she lives in a bustling Arkansas town near her family. In between writing books, she enjoys painting and playing the piano.

Blanche specializes in clean mysteries that have middle-aged women protagonists with a tendency to become involved in strange and mysterious happenings in their hometowns.

Darcy Campbell, retired newspaper reporter, and her mother Flora Tucker, protagonists, can't stay out of trouble in Levi, Oklahoma. On the surface, this lovely town seems tranquil, filled with law-abiding and peaceful people. As Darcy and Flora discover, more is going on than meets the eye. *The Cemetery Club, Grave Shift, Best Left Buried,* and *Grave Heritage* follow these courageous women from one harrowing adventure to another.

The second series, the Ned McNeil Moonlight books, begins with Nettie Elizabeth McNeil returning to her hometown of Ednalee, looking forward to a reunion with her only living relative, her Uncle Javin. The reunion fails to happen and Ned, as her friends call her, discovers that she is involved in a web of lies and mysteries that have their origin in a murder that happened decades ago. *Moonlight Can Be Murder* indeed. More excitement takes place under a full moon in *By the Fright of the Silvery Moon*. The third Ned McNeil book, *Moonstruck and Murderous*, follows Ned and her two childhood friends into the mystery surrounding a 200-year-old house that is lovely to look at but is built around a deadly secret of its own.

VISIT BLANCHE AT:

Website and blog: www.BlancheDayManos.com

Facebook: BlancheDayManos.Author

Dear Readers,
If you enjoyed this
book enough to review
it for Goodreads, B&N,
or Amazon.com, I'd
appreciate it!
Thanks, Blanche

Find more great reads at
Pen-L.com

Made in the USA
Coppell, TX
30 May 2021

56560526R00125